Praise for Kerka

"This sparkling combination
bound to enc
—*Kirkus Reviews*

"Excellent. . . . The writing is refreshingly well done
and weaves together the author's knowledge of art,
folklore, and botany to paint a magical world where
readers' senses are piqued by the likes of stone fairies,
cave anemones, and a queen named Patchouli."
—*SLJ*

"Great for girls who love fairies and magical worlds."
—KidzWorld.com

Praise for *Birdie's Book*

"Bozarth's tale is a beguiling mix of magic, adventure
and eco-awareness, and her message of girl-power and
positive change will resonate with tween readers."
—*Kirkus Reviews*

"A fun, light read that ought to be a hit with girls who
like adventure and magic."
—Books for Kids (blog)

"Bozarth has taken the best aspects of various young
adult genres and mixed them together in a fresh and
optimistic way."
—Kidsreads.com

The Fairy Godmother Academy

The Fairy Godmother Academy

BOOK 4

Lilu's Book

Jan Bozarth

A YEARLING BOOK

Copyright © 2011 by FGA Media Inc.

All rights reserved. Published in the United States by Yearling, an imprint of Random House Children's Books, a division of Random House, Inc., New York.

Yearling and the jumping horse design are registered trademarks of Random House, Inc.

Visit us on the Web! www.randomhouse.com/kids

Educators and librarians, for a variety of teaching tools, visit us at www.randomhouse.com/teachers

Join the Fairy Godmother Academy!
FairyGodmotherAcademy.com

Library of Congress Cataloging-in-Publication Data
Bozarth, Jan.
Lilu's book / Jan Bozarth. — 1st Yearling ed.
p. cm. — (The Fairy Godmother Academy ; bk. 4)
Summary: After waking to find herself in Aventurine—the place where girls train to become fairy godmothers—an African American twin sister who is afraid of discovering her own uniqueness embarks on her first mission to rescue a special bird's egg before a devastating magical hurricane hits.
ISBN 978-0-375-85187-2 (pbk.) — ISBN 978-0-375-95187-9 (lib. bdg.) — ISBN 978-0-375-89336-0 (ebook)
[1. Fairy godmothers—Fiction. 2. Fairies—Fiction. 3. Twins—Fiction.
4. Sisters—Fiction. 5. Magic—Fiction. 6. African Americans—Fiction.] I. Title.
PZ7.B6974Li 2011
[Fic]—dc22
2011002717

Printed in the United States of America
10 9 8 7 6 5 4 3 2 1
First Yearling Edition 2011

For my twins, Evan and Dustin

Contents

1

Twisting Somersault

My heart pounded in my ears as I climbed the ladder to the diving board, pulled myself up, and stood staring out at everything and nothing. Up there, it was like standing at the top of the world.

Corny, right? But absolutely true.

The sky was bone white. I felt as if I were close enough to touch it, and I could almost smell the lightning on that hot and humid July day. Electrified lightning bolts are not a diver's friend. Still, being there calmed my nerves and gave me a sense of peace. The whole top-of-the-world thing, I meant that, honestly. Being on the three-meter springboard makes me feel like no one can touch me—like I'm magical or something.

Diving does that to me, makes me all loopy and sentimental. My dad had gotten my sister and me

1

interested in competitive swimming. We learned to swim long before preschool. By kindergarten we were competitive swimmers and expert snorkelers. Then when we were ten, he signed us up for a springboard diving program.

That was the same year he and Mom split up.

Block it out, Lilu!

I was about to make my final dive at the junior dive competition in Charleston, South Carolina. No stray thoughts about how many crazy changes were happening to my family should break my focus. No time to worry about how Mom was taking us away from South Carolina to New York City to "start our new lives."

My heart was doing dives of its own. I reminded it to take it easy, thank you very much. A girl can't exactly plan the most perfect, most amazing, most essential dive of her life when her heart is trying to send her straight to the emergency room.

Did kids my age have heart attacks?

Mom said watching so much television had turned me into a hypochondriac — you know, a person who always thinks she's got some kind of disease. But everybody knew I would much rather watch animal shows than doctor shows — well, most of the time.

See, my dad teaches marine biology at a local

college, and my mom makes documentaries. They used to work together on her short films about endangered marine species. The whole family went everywhere together and did everything together.

"You can do it, baby! Keep your focus!" It was my mom's voice.

Sweat trickled down my cheeks, and I felt my bronzed skin burn with embarrassment. Mom was like that, though. She'd give a shout-out to her "babies" no matter what. Didn't she know I wasn't a baby anymore?

Still, I couldn't quite clear my head. So much was at stake. This was the most important dive of my life!

At least, I hoped so. I wanted this one dive to change all of our lives. Like in the hopelessly hokey teen movies where everything the characters have ever dreamt comes down to this one moment, this one terrific scene.

That's what I wanted: because for me, a perfect dive would fix my life.

Maybe . . . maybe if I could become the junior champion today, then my twin sister, Tandy, would get excited about diving again. And if that crazy wish were granted, then maybe my even crazier wish for Mom to change her mind about moving could be granted, too.

And maybe if we stay here and don't move . . . Well, Mom and Dad might get back together! My craziest wish of all.

A whistle shrieked. Muscles in my stomach tightened. Showtime.

Desire. Dedication. Determination.

Coach Regina drilled that into us. She got the idea to start a dive team for kids our age — I joined her team when I was ten; I'm thirteen now — after she began coaching at the high school. She said if kids learned the fundamentals of springboard diving earlier, they'd be better equipped for high school competition.

Time for my final dive — a free dive. They're the most difficult. Mine was a combination of a forward straight dive with a half twist. For young divers, it could either make you look like you were one step closer to the Olympics or headed for . . . dive failure.

Trust me, no one wants dive failure. That's just one step above belly flop. A belly flop might be funny in your aunt's pool on the Fourth of July, but trust me, in front of strict-faced judges, your family, and coaches, belly flops rate right up there with pulled groin muscles!

My heart somersaulted. I took two quick strides down the board. I scrubbed my toes against the bumpy surface of the springboard, feeling the familiar scratch from the same spot where I always stood to start my run.

Desire. Dedication. Determination.

"Go, Lilu!"

A chorus of "shhh"s sprayed through the thick, chlorine-scented air. This time it was Tandy's voice. I could sense the stern looks my twin was getting. People would worry that she'd interrupted my flow. But Tandy's verbal push was just what I needed.

Starting position . . . approach . . . takeoff . . . flight . . . entry.

I pushed everything else from my mind. I'd found my favorite starting position and began my approach.

Then my whole brain went to my knees. On the takeoff, it was all about the knees. Let them get lazy and you don't get enough height. Don't get enough height and—*SPLASH!*—dive over.

My arms swung upward at the same time as my knees began to bend. With all my strength, my stomach muscles tightened to help pull my knees up as high as possible.

I heard the familiar thunk of the board as I felt

myself leave it in a small bounce to gather momentum. Now it was just me and the board and the smell of the air. No fans. No coaches. No parents or sisters or "new futures."

Just me and the board.

As soon as my knees were perpendicular to my body, I pulled my toes back to the end of the board. My arms were straight. My fingertips stretched toward the sky. Hips and shoulders straight and facing forward.

Then I was off the board and springing toward heaven.

My arm came around to twist my straight body in the air.

My toes stayed together as I twisted toward the water.

At the last second, I brought my hands together over my head. My left hand clasped my right with palms flat, creating a pocket of air for my rip entry as I cleaved through the water into a silent world of aqua blue.

I broke the surface and took a breath. Everyone was on their feet.

I did it! I did it!

Quickly, I swam toward the side of the pool, my eyes searching the stands. Mom and Dad were sitting together. They'd been like that all day. But where was Tandy? She had been right there.

"You did it, kiddo! Great job!" Coach Regina wrapped a towel around me and patted me enthusiastically on the back. "That was the best dive you've ever had!" She hugged me and I hugged her, and it was all great until I saw Tandy.

She was out of the bleachers, standing near the tunnel, her cell phone pressed to her ear. What would make her call someone or even take a call when I was on the verge of making my most spectacular dive ever? I was working myself up when she turned, saw me staring, and raced over. Before I could even say a word, she blurted, *"Cucimita!"*

I was still toweling myself, trying to catch my breath, the slight taste of chlorine in my mouth. I frowned. It must be something big–Tandy was using our secret language.

"You have great news?" I asked.

"I got the part, Lilu! I did it. When we move to New York, I'm going to be in my first *real* musical."

Cucimita! I thought. I just had the dive of my life. The dive that was supposed to change our lives. And instead of it being so amazing that Tandy would rejoin me on the dive team, she was off plotting her big acting career.

By the time the judges' scores were up and the winning ribbon was placed on my neck, sharp pellets of rain began to fall. Mom and Dad raced with us toward the parking lot. My ribbon felt wonderful. Then Dad had this "Way to go, baby girl" expression on his face that turned sad when he looked at Mom and saw she was already pulling away from him in the rain.

I wanted to yell "Cut!" This scene wasn't supposed to go this way. By now, the way I'd pictured it, we were supposed to be in a heartwarming group hug, vowing to try to put our family back together. The only thing that would be missing was a dog.

The medal suddenly felt heavy. Dad hugged me good-bye, and then Mom, Tandy, and I scrambled soaking wet into Mom's car. All the way home, in between calling and texting everyone she knew with her great news, Tandy sang. Watching me win the meet had done nothing to make my sister miss diving. She was already looking toward a future I wished was far, far away.

"Lilu, wait!" yelled Tandy.

But I was moving, sliding across the seat and out of the car before Mom really had a chance to stop.

"Sorry," I called over my shoulder, face down to

keep the rain out of my eyes. To keep Tandy from seeing that I was upset when I shouldn't be upset, which would mean explaining why I was upset, which I couldn't because I didn't fully understand it. "I've got a headache. I just need to lay down."

I heard one car door slam shut, then another. Buckets of rain poured over us. Only a few seconds had passed, and already I was soaked again.

Tandy touched my elbow before we reached the front of the house. "Lilu? You okay?"

Thunder crackled. Wind gusted from the ocean and drove the rain right into our faces. It was like staring into a blurred mirror. She was my reflection, only different.

"Fine," I said.

"C'mon, girls! We've got to get out of this rain!"

I flew up the stairs, filled with a dozen different emotions. How could I be so dense? I'd really made myself believe that winning a stupid medal in a stupid dive meet could change our stupid lives back to the way they used to be. Back when my twin sister and I did everything together and my mom and dad were one family. But here I was, sidestepping packing boxes on the stairs, racing to my bedroom, feeling like a total moron on what should have been the happiest day of my life.

I won. That should be enough to make me happy. Right?

I peeled off my wet clothes, pulled on dry shorts and a tank top, flopped on top of the covers, and immediately fell asleep.

Hours later when I awakened, I was holding my medal between my fingers. The storm had stopped, and the air coming through the window was soft as a lullaby.

"You feel up to some dinner?" Mom appeared in the doorway. She was using her quiet voice. That's what Tan and I called it. Whenever either one of us had done something dumb or had had an "emotional" day we could count on Mom to go all Oprah on us.

Funny how often the soft, let-me-be-your-best-friend voice worked, soothing us and helping us to feel like whatever had happened was not the end of the world. The light shone behind her from the hallway, and through the pale lavender curtains in my room I could see that the sky had gone completely dark.

"Sure, Mom," I said, rolling out of my bed. "I'll be right down." She disappeared behind the door. It took a few minutes for me to get my bearings. With all the daylight drained from the sky, purplish twilight covered every surface.

I had to bypass several large cardboard boxes to make it from the stairs to the dining room. Packing was a pain in the butt. I never realized how many boxes it took to start a new life. Each cardboard box, neatly taped and labeled, contained bits and pieces of our lives. Like a puzzle being carefully taken apart.

It was hard to believe that this time next month we'd be living in New York City. We'd spent our whole lives right here on the shore in South Carolina.

Tandy loved the idea of living in the city. She wanted to be a star, and she joked about becoming a huge success on Broadway.

Not me.

I'd always believed my life was in the sea. I wanted to be a marine biologist like Dad or a marine animal veterinarian at an aquarium.

Tandy couldn't wait to move. I couldn't think about moving without my insides getting all squishy. But to the world, we looked like the exact same person.

In the dining room, Tandy was setting the table and singing again. She looked so happy. Of course I was happy for her. I just hated how much it made me feel like we were going in opposite directions. When the phone rang from the other side of the kitchen door, she looked up.

We heard Mom giggle like a schoolgirl. "I'll get it," she sang out.

Tandy and I exchanged looks. No doubt the caller ID had flashed on the tiny television screen in the kitchen. It was Him. Our future stepdad.

Tandy nodded toward the kitchen. "The two of them are going to need supervision once we're all living up there," she said with a wink.

I tried to answer with something clever. We gave our mom a playfully hard time about George, the guy she was marrying in the fall. But the truth was, he made her happy. They'd been keeping a long-distance relationship going for months. Now Mom finally had the chance to produce a children's television show in New York for a national market. Something she'd been wanting to do for as long as I could remember.

"She'll be all right," I said. How lame was that?

"So, are you okay? Is your headache gone?" Tandy put a large salad bowl filled with greens, chunks of bright red tomato, and slivers of crisp yellow onion in the center of the table. Beside it, she placed a handmade basket filled with warm rolls. I remembered when Mom had made that basket.

My insides clenched all over again.

"What? What's wrong?" asked Tandy.

"Nothing's wrong," I lied. I'm a terrible liar and don't know why I try.

"You're a terrible liar, Lilu. I don't know why you try. Spill it." Tandy and I usually could tell what the other's thinking—it's a twin thing. She was born sixteen minutes and eleven seconds before me, though, so technically, that made her the older sister.

I rolled my eyes and pretended she couldn't push me around with her "I'm the oldest so you'd better do as I say" routine.

But Tandy stepped closer and placed her hand on my wrist, touching the ocean-blue bracelet there. We'd braided enough bracelets for all the girls on our dive team. *My* dive team, since Tandy quit this year. Even though we could have made close to eighty bucks if we'd sold them all, we gave them to the team as gifts.

Aurantiado.

Tandy didn't say the word aloud, but I felt it through her skin. I knew she was saying it, speaking our language. *Aurantiado* was based on the *marginella aurantia* shell found in Senegal—the shell we were studying when Mom told us about the divorce.

"I'm not troubled," I said, responding to our word's secret meaning. "You worry too much." I spun around, hoping to avoid her gaze. I removed three beige linen napkins from the sideboard, rolled them, and slipped each inside a hand-carved ring. Then I placed one napkin beside each dinner plate.

Tandy hadn't moved.

Oh, man, she drove me nuts when she did that.

"Tan, cut it out!" I said.

Aurantiado.

"Nothing's bothering me," I said.

"Aurantiado!" said Tandy. This time no twin telepathy needed.

I sighed, then picked up the basket.

Tandy looked at me, not understanding.

I said, "Remember when Mom made this basket? It was the first time she tried teaching us the family tradition of weaving."

Tandy shrugged. "Of course I remember," she said. "That's when we started our business with the baskets, bracelets, and seashell necklaces."

"Do you remember how easy it was for you to follow along and how hard it was for me?"

Tandy put her hands on her hips and shook her head. "No, I don't remember that."

"C'mon, Tandy. We couldn't have been more than seven at the time. This stuff." I swept my hand around, turning slowly, indicating all the family treasures made by my mother and our ancestors—

tightly woven baskets, loosely bound place mats with beads or other adornments added to the dried grasses and reeds, lap blankets crocheted with organic yarns for cool winter nights on the beach. My mother was like her mother and her mother before her, a whiz at working with her hands.

Tandy caught on easily. Me, not so much.

"Lilu, you're *great* with the bracelets. And animals. And seashells. Think of all the money you've raised to donate to save the sea turtles, the whooping cranes, everything. We're selling tons of crafts—stuff we *both* made—thanks to the website George set up."

George was some sort of business guru. Tandy was right; thanks to him, we'd sold a lot more bracelets and crafts online than we'd ever sold at the craft fairs. We made a great team, my sister and I. She didn't get it, though. I wasn't going this nutso over baskets or bracelets or websites.

It was *us*. Her and me. It was like we were being pulled apart by some enormous tide. Like when we finally made it to shore, we'd be in two separate places, and I'd be all alone.

My sister huffed and rolled her eyes. "Hello! Baby sister, are you in there?"

It was my turn for an eye roll.

"Who cares if you can't weave a basket as well as

someone else?" said Tandy. "Are you really going to be a basket weaver when you grow up? I don't know how many Olympic divers also need to know how to make baskets, so I think you're good." Tandy took the basket from my hands and tugged me into a hug.

I clung to her for a second, then pulled away. My face felt warm. I was being a dope again. "So, tell me all about this musical you're going to be in. . . ."

"We'll always be 'us,' Little LeeLee."

She caught me off guard. Maybe being born sixteen minutes earlier really did make a big difference. LeeLee. She hadn't called me that since we were little.

Tandy grinned. "Stop being so mopey and dramatic, you little dope. I'm your big sister. I'm here for you."

She pushed me toward the kitchen. "Now stop acting so serious, and go help Mom in the kitchen."

I turned and snapped off a military salute to her. "Yes, ma'am!" I said.

When I pushed through the kitchen door, Mom was standing at the counter, pulling back the aluminum foil from the roasted chicken. The room filled with the scent of lemon pepper, fresh basil and oregano from our garden, and the delicious warm and sweet scent of citrus. It was Mom's famous citrus roast. Beautiful circles of sliced orange and lemon covered the chicken's crisp golden skin.

"Mom, that smells delicious!"

She gave me a sideways glance, then smiled. "You always did love this to death." Then she turned away from the chicken and stared carefully at my face. It was like she was trying to memorize it—or look for something.

"Why are you looking at me like that?" I asked.

She gave a little laugh. "Sorry, kiddo. It's just . . ."

For several *looooong* seconds she was silent, and it freaked me out. Why was she looking at me like she had never seen me before? She took a deep breath, then let it out slowly.

"Lilu, I know you know, but I can't help saying it anyway: I love you girls very, very much. You two are the meaning to my whole world."

Uh-oh! We were definitely headed toward an Awkward Emotional Moment. When we were about eight, whenever Mom got this look on her face, we'd yell, "Oh no! Mom is trying to bond!" Then we'd run shrieking through the house.

She hugged me tight.

"Mom, let go. You're going to break me!" I wanted to lighten the moment. Could she sense how confused and conflicted I'd been feeling about all the changes in our lives?

"Lilu, I know you've been pretty conflicted about all the changes going on," she said.

I swear, it's like she and Tandy have some sort of probe in my brain that tells them exactly what I'm thinking.

"Mom, I'm fine."

"After dinner, when your sister goes to babysit, you and I are going to sit on the back porch and have some time for ourselves."

I felt my eyebrows crinkle into question marks. In the stainless steel fridge, I saw my reflection distort, like in a fun-house mirror. My mother laughed. Then she pulled me into another hug.

"Mom! I'm at that age when too many hugs is just plain embarrassing. Can you please just tell me what's up? Tan and I have talked to you about unauthorized bonding."

"You guys . . ." Tandy pushed through the kitchen door and saw Mom still hugging me and me trying to break free. "Uh-oh!" she shrieked. "Unauthorized bonding!"

We all started running around like crazy people, through the kitchen and into the dining room. Mom was making kissy sounds and yelling, "I need someone to hug!"

Finally, Tandy was laughing so hard she dropped

to the floor and said, "Stop! I'm starving. Less bonding, more eating."

"Be right there," Mom said. Then she added, "Tandy, go outside and get us a few fresh hydrangeas from the bush by the front door." She whispered to me, "Shhh! Just girl talk. For us!"

"Hmm . . . if you say so," I replied with an exaggerated eye roll.

She pinched my cheek, and I knew what was coming next—as soon as Tan left to babysit our cousin, also known as Problem Child, Mom was going to sit me down and engage in the itchiest of feel-good experiences: bonding.

I'd need to keep an eye on her. Especially if she wanted me to talk about my feelings from earlier.

How embarrassing would that be? Telling Mom I was having movie-of-the-week fantasies about our family getting back together. That kind of thing could get a girl into trouble.

2

Secrets of the Shell

Despite the warning lights and alarms going off inside my brain, I managed to enjoy dinner. It was delicious. The three of us talked about a bit of everything.

Mom was talking a mile a minute. She got like that when she was nervous or amped up. "I can't wait to see you girls all dressed up as bridesmaids," she said.

So this might sound a bit crazy, but as much as I fantasized about Mom and Dad getting back together, I was really looking forward to my mom's wedding and wearing that totally beautiful blue dress with the tiny white and pink flowers at the waist.

Would it totally stink if Mom and George got married just for the ceremony, then we came back here to live with Dad again? (I'm guessing George would have some real issues with that plan!)

"I've set aside some pretty seashells that we can use like beads to decorate our headbands," I said.

When Mom smiled at me, it was like seeing the sun rise. I couldn't remember seeing her more beautiful — or happy.

Was she really that happy to be moving away from her old life?

My aunt Mary rang the doorbell while we were clearing the table. Tandy grabbed her iPod and raced for the door. She paused and asked, "LeeLee, sure you don't want to come with?" She flicked her eyebrows up and down.

I glanced over and saw Mom's face tighten. She really didn't want me to go. Why?

"Nah, I'd better stay here," I said. "You know Problem Child is no fan of mine."

"Uh, Lilu, maybe if you stopped calling him Problem Child it'd help."

I shook my head. "Um, no, I don't think it would."

"Well, see you in a few hours. Later!" And she was gone.

Mom and I finished putting the dirty dishes in the dishwasher and wiping down the counters. Then Mom suggested we get some dessert and something cool to drink and go sit on the back porch.

The alarms started blaring again.

"Mom, I'm still tired from this afternoon. Maybe I should—"

"Nonsense!" She cut me off. "Now help me with our after-dinner treat."

A few minutes later, we headed for the back porch. Holding two large glasses filled with iced tea steeped with fresh peach and sprigs of fresh mint, I sat on the metal swing next to Mom. The back porch was screened and faced the ocean. The sky was dark, but the clouds from earlier had cleared. A full moon was hanging low over the ocean.

Mom handed me a plate with a slice of sweet potato pie, and I gave her a glass of tea and then took a big sip from mine. The tea smelled fresh, strong, sweet . . . but it couldn't compare with the overwhelming scent of the ocean.

The back porch was my favorite part of the house. At the other end was a futon with an over-sized cushion covered in fat blue and white stripes. I'd slept out here a number of times, and I always woke up feeling refreshed.

Three sides of the porch were screened, and the one wall was lined with antique shelves. Each shelf held baskets and jars filled with seashells. Our seashell collection was also strung together and hung around the room.

"You were terrific today at the pool," said Mom.

I shrugged. Sitting so close to her, feeling the warmth of her skin, I felt cozy and safe. "The best part, I think, was seeing you in the stands next to Dad."

Oh no! That just slipped out! I'm such a dope. This is exactly the type of thing moms are looking for when they set us up for special bonding time.

She turned toward me, and the swing creaked. "You miss him a lot, don't you?"

I dropped my head back and let out a long sigh. "Mom," I groaned. "I know you guys aren't getting back together. And I know it's not my fault or our fault like some kids think. And I know you're very happy, okay?"

"Well, sounds like you've got it all figured out. Eat your pie, sweetheart," Mom said.

I took a large forkful of the creamy sweet potato pie. "Mom, this is delicious. You know I could eat sweet potato pie every day!"

Mom set her plate on her lap and turned toward me. Her eyes studied me for a second, and then she said, "How about you and Tandy? Everything okay?"

Moms have that way about them, you know. They're more than smart—they're clever. Here she was letting me talk about her and Dad and everything, then out of nowhere she hits me with what's really bugging me. I guess thinking I could hide it from her was silly. Mom always figures things out.

Still, if I had any chance of avoiding more mother-daughter bonding, I had to rely on the one trick in every kid's book: denial. "Mom, me and Tan are fine. *I'm* fine. Really."

"So you're telling me you're excited about moving and delighted with all the changes and ecstatic that your sister is developing other interests and is not spending as much time with you?" she asked.

I studied the pie on my plate and pushed a piece of crust back and forth. "I . . ." My voice broke. I tried to say something lighthearted, but it just got caught in my throat.

She reached over and squeezed my knee. "Lilu, baby, having you girls has been a constant blessing, a gift. I've watched you two blossom, watched your friendship, your special connection. I've watched it and loved it. But I know the two of you are at an age when you might not be quite as identical as you once were. Tandy is getting really involved in her singing and acting. She's great at it. But I see the way you get whenever that stuff comes up. I guess what I want to say to you is don't be afraid to let her go.

Once you let her go, you give yourself permission to be all that *Lilu* was meant to be. You are a rare and beautiful person, Lilu Hart. Don't be afraid of your uniqueness."

Nothing to do with a speech like that but eat a few forkfuls of pie and let it sink in. Mom hummed while she ate. The tall, lush sweetgrass and foxtail alongside the house swished and swayed in the wind, lending a backup chorus.

"This is for you." Mom held out her hand, and the moonlight flitted over the object in her outstretched palm.

It was a shell unlike any I'd ever seen. I reached out and took it from her. "It looks like a crescent moon," I said.

Mom nodded, her half smile now almost hidden behind her forkful of pie.

"Hey, Mom, have you packed all the old seashell books? I'd love to look this one up. It's amazing!"

She set her plate on the floor, lifted her iced tea, and took a long swallow. Then she said, "It *is* amazing, Lilu. But you won't find it in any book. It is one of a kind, made by the sea and the moon specifically for our people, our ancestors, and passed down from generation to generation."

"Like the baskets?" I squeezed my hand shut,

pressing the cool, unusual shell into my skin. Then my hand opened wide as my mind whirred with the fear of damaging something so precious.

"Sort of like the baskets. But the crescent moon came before the baskets. Without the pure magic of this moon's light, our family might never have found its way, would never have understood its purpose."

I frowned. "You're talking about Aventurine again, aren't you?"

"Let's take a walk," she said.

The screen door snapped shut like a turtle's mouth. As we moved toward the ocean, I glanced over my shoulder. Our house was candy pink with big, rolled tiles on the roof. Black shutters sat beside the windows. On nights like tonight, after a huge afternoon storm, we opened the windows to allow the ocean air inside.

An occasional strong gust of wind blew from the ocean, making me glad that I had used a red scarf as a headband to keep my unruly hair out of my face.

Mom led me to a jagged rock formation and began to climb. We were careful to place our feet in the crags and craters, moving carefully until we reached a lip of the rock face that flattened. With my eyes closed, I filled my lungs with the beautiful ocean scent, fresh and briny and alive. Whenever I was this close to the ocean, especially at night, it became a symphony in my head.

Mom interrupted my thoughts. "Lilu, you know your aunt Mary and I have talked a lot about Aventurine with you girls over the years."

I nodded.

"Well, now it's your time," she said. "I didn't know which of you girls would be first, but now I know it's you."

"Mom, you've always talked about Aventurine; you talk about it being such a cool, magical place. A place for strong women to figure out who they are and train to become fairy godmothers. . . ."

"That's right."

"So . . . it's real? I thought it was just some sort of bedtime story."

Mom's laughter was deep and sweet. "No, baby, that was no bedtime story. Aventurine is definitely real."

My knees buckled. My hand shut tight, and the shell dug painfully into my palm.

"Whoa!" Mom reached out and grabbed me. She helped me sit on the flat part of the craggy rock and didn't take her arms from around me until I was sitting, facing the ocean, feeling the dampness of the surf against my skin.

"Umm, maybe next time you share life-changing news with me, we can do it someplace more stable? Remember, I'm the one who isn't that good with change!"

"Don't worry, Lilu. You'll be fine." Mom squeezed my shoulder, and I let myself lean into her.

Then she lightly tapped the fist I was squeezing the shell in. "Relax," she said. "You won't lose it. When you need it, it will find you. Aventurine will teach you how to use it."

I frowned again. This was crazy!

Mom smiled. "I'm going to ask for a favor."

"What is it?"

When she looked at me, she took my hands in hers and said, "I want you to stop thinking so hard about how everything should be and what pieces should go where."

Now it was my turn to smile. She had me. I sighed. "Okay, Mom. So, tell me again about Aventurine. Remind me how this is supposed to work."

"Early on, I knew I was blessed with the gift of weaving stories," she said.

"I thought our family's skill is weaving baskets," I said.

"Those are skills passed down from generation to generation. Skills that, if you believe in yourself and have faith, you, too, can develop. Or maybe you'll develop other skills that work just as well. But my true 'gift,' that thing I knew I was meant to do more than anything else, that was writing screenplays for movies and television. It was what I'd dreamed of since I was a little girl. Writing allows me to speak with people in their language. Not the language of their ears, but the language of their hearts.

"Our family comes from the Songa Lineage. Crafting a story isn't so different from crafting a basket. Instead of sturdy reeds, I take words out of the air and shape them into thoughts and emotions."

I nodded. I hadn't thought of it that way.

"So," I said, "what is the Songo Lineage thing about?"

"The Songa Lineage. When famine threatened our ancestors' survival in Africa, our queen spoke to the moon."

"And the moon spoke back?" I asked.

Mom smiled again, her teeth as white as the shell. "More like the moon goddess. It turns out the moon needed us, too. It had gone off track and pulled the tides out of alignment. Our great ancestor, a woman known as Mama Akuko, herself a fairy godmother, saved the moon and the tides."

When I just stared at her, Mom said, "In some

African languages, *akuko* means 'youngest twin.' "

My jaw dropped. "We have ancestors who were twins?"

"Of course," Mom said. "You know twin genes run in certain families. If you're a twin, there's a good chance you have ancestors who were twins."

"What did Mama Akuko do for the moon?"

"Mama Akuko was an expert weaver. So expert that she found a way to tug the moonbeams and guide the tides back on course."

"But how?" I asked.

"Well, my love, that is a secret that stays with Mama Akuko and the moon goddess, a secret you must earn," she said.

Something in her posture was so . . . *real.* The angle of her body, the tilt of her head, the way her shoulders pulled back.

"How . . . how will I do that? Earn the secret, I mean. And what if I can't do what it takes?" My voice faltered on that last part.

Then, before Mom could answer my questions, I hit her with another: "Why me and not Tandy?"

"This is about you, the youngest twin."

More questions rushed at me, but Mom held up

a finger. "Shhh," she said. "I know you have questions, and I know you have much to learn. Keep the shell with you tonight; keep it near you while you sleep. Don't worry about finding Aventurine. Aventurine will find you!"

With that, she stood and took my hand.

We walked without speaking, down the craggy rock face, across the moonlit sand, toward our candy-pink beach house. With the ocean's music rushing at our backs and the moon elongating our shadows—and lighting our path.

3

Underwater Dreaming

I was awake in bed when Tandy returned from
babysitting. As usual, she turned on the overhead light
and practically baked my corneas.

"Hey!" I cried. "I'm trying to sleep over here."

She yawned. "Sorry, sis. I'm so tired. I think
maybe you're right. Maybe your cousin *is* a problem
child. That kid practically killed me tonight."

My arm was flung over my face. I slid it aside
and peeked out. "Told you."

Tandy had a regular bedtime routine. No matter
how tired she was. No matter how late it was. No
matter how long I'd been asleep or trying to fall asleep,
Tandy's nighttime ritual was the same:

Five minutes of yoga on the rug next to her bed.

Two minutes of singing the musical scales.

Kiss her fingertips and gently tap the glass of the

aquarium as she says good-night to our fish.

Brush her teeth for three minutes.

Smile into the mirror.

Floss.

Then wash her face and apply night cream.

And since she was afraid of the dark, she turned on as many lights as possible for this ordeal.

By the time she got to the night-cream-on-her-face part I had covered *my* face with the pillow. "Please, Tan. My eyes! Shut off the light. I'm tired, too."

Finally, she clicked off the lights in the bedroom and bathroom. She'd flung her clothes into a heap on the floor and had pulled a nightgown out of another pile. By now, every movement annoyed me. Her bed creaked. Her sheets rustled.

"Tandy Joella Hart, if you don't—"

"Okay, okay . . . geez. You know I have to squirm around to get comfortable. Chill!"

At that, we both let out great, long sighs. Right away I felt bad for griping but didn't say anything. Not at first, anyway.

But after half an hour or so, I raised my arm off my face and squinted at her in the dark. "Tan?"

"Hmm?"

"You having trouble falling asleep, too?"

"Mmm-hmm."

We were both silent for a while longer; then I had another one of my moments where what I was thinking just popped right out. "Hey, Tan?"

I heard her head turn on her pillow. In the semi-darkness, with the aquarium light throwing wiggly shadows, her face faded in and out. She waited in silence, so I plunged ahead. "You don't miss diving at all?"

I felt her staring at me from across the room. "What are you really trying to get at?"

"Um—"

She didn't let me answer. "I miss hanging out with you, but, you know what? Acting is my thing. I love it so much, Lilu. When I'm onstage, singing or whatever, it's like I'm alive for the very first time."

I made a noise like the air had been socked out of me.

"What?" she said.

"That's how I used to feel when we did stuff together. That's how I used to feel when we were on the same swim team and dive team. When we both tried to outdo each other with ways to save the oceans."

"Face it, Lilu, the ocean-saving stuff has always been more your thing than our thing."

"No way! You were totally into it," I shot back.

"Because at the time, it was all I knew. We had

a lot of cool adventures with Mom and Dad doing all that stuff—learning about the sea and rushing out to the beach every time Dad heard about a beached whale or whatever. Then I got a part in the school play . . . Well, it was like I had found *me*."

My talk with Mom about Aventurine came to mind. Being onstage helped Tandy discover her uniqueness. "Is it that important for you to be so different? From me, I mean?" I asked.

Her mattress springs creaked. She had turned onto her side and propped herself up with her elbow. We faced each other in the glowy darkness, shadows floating across the grayness between us.

"You're stronger than you think," she said.

"That doesn't answer my question. Does it really mean that much to you to be so different, so unique from me?"

She let out a long breath. "Lilu, you're so good at so many things and you have such a strong personality, sometimes I feel like if I'm not careful, I won't be a whole person. I'll just be, like, some miniversion of you."

"Tan, you're the strong one. You're the one—"

"Lilu, one day you're going to see what I see. Trust me, you don't need me as much as you think you do. You really don't!"

With that, we both flopped back onto our

pillows. My eyes began to burn with sleepiness. I was so tired, my mind couldn't quite process what Tandy had said. She thought I was the strong personality? Even as I felt sleep dragging me down its undertow, I couldn't help wondering, *If I'm so strong, why do I feel so . . . lost?*

I had that feeling in my ears: the feeling of being underwater, down at the bottom of the deepest part of the pool—the area right under the diving boards. I opened my eyes, and I *was* underwater! But not in a pool, no; this was definitely a deep freshwater lake. I was resting at the bottom, much deeper than I would normally ever dare to go. It was eerie. But sort of cool, too, you know?

I've had dreams that left me feeling anxious or weird or sad or whatever. Not this time. I felt like I could sit there forever watching the animal and plant life. Even though it was dark and cold this far down, there was at least some light streaming through the lacy seaweed.

Wait, how was I not freaking out? Shouldn't I be drowning right about now?

I kicked off frantically with all the power I could muster, and then something really strange happened— I automatically took a deep breath.

Air!

I blew out a stream of dancing bubbles and took one more quick breath as a test. It still worked! I could actually breathe underwater. This had to be the coolest dream ever.

Now that I wasn't desperately trying to reach the surface, I could look around. I was wearing a bright purple wet suit and water shoes. The kind of outfit I liked to wear when I went snorkeling in shallow water. Only this wet suit wasn't made out of normal material; it was glowing a little, but it definitely hadn't been glowing when I was further down in the dark. Weird.

Mom did this educational TV show once on something called bioluminescence—which is when living organisms glow. It's really cool, and there are lots of theories and myths about why it happens. Maybe my wet suit was bioluminescent or something.

I was right in the thick of the lush seaweed, which kept tickling me—almost like it was doing it on purpose—so I swam up higher and noticed that my wet suit glowed a little bit more. I turned to my left and started swimming to check out more of my surroundings.

As always, being in any kind of water made me feel relaxed and happy. This lake was teeming with life, and I wanted to investigate some strange-looking fish up ahead. They seemed to disappear and reappear in different places. I'd never seen camouflage that good.

As I neared the school of fish, they winked off. But I had gotten close enough to see that they looked a lot like swordfish, with sharp, rapier-like noses that I was going to have to watch out for. They were much more brightly colored than swordfish, though, with deep red and bright yellow stripes. If they really were swordfish, they would have been a plain gray or bluish color, and they wouldn't be traveling in a school in freshwater; they'd have been out on their own in the ocean.

Suddenly they winked back on—completely surrounding me! How did they do that without me noticing? They must be just as curious about this big purpley glowing fish in their neighborhood as I was about them. But I wasn't glowing anymore. Why did my wet suit decide to turn off?

The winkfish—that's what I decided to call them—swam around me in a circle and then seemed to have had enough of investigating me. They disappeared just as quickly as they had appeared. And I had no idea how they went from being right in front of my face to completely gone. It was like magic.

I felt a sting on my hand, then my neck. I swatted at my skin like I was trying to crush a pesky mosquito but completely missed whatever was biting me.

Bright sparks of gold started shooting by my face. I turned to see where they were coming from, and a tsunami of little fish hit out of nowhere. Each fish sent a jolt of electricity into me as it brushed by. Luckily my wet suit covered most of my body; only my hands, neck, face, and ankles were unprotected. But, man, did they hurt!

Swimming against them would've been a really bad idea, so I started swimming as fast as I could with the golden current, using just my feet and legs. With my hands pinned against my body, I avoided hitting more of the painful little guys, but they were still nipping at my ankles and stinging my face. I was barely managing to keep up but was suddenly grateful for all of the laps that Coach made us do.

The sparkfish—another name I just came up with—were taking me closer to shore. I thought this might be the right way to go, because my wet suit began to glow brighter and brighter as we neared the shallows.

When we reached an area where I could almost touch the ground, the school swerved to the right and continued on. It dawned on me that a school of fish wouldn't be moving that fast unless a predator was in the area, so I looked back over my shoulder.

Out of the deep I could see a shape getting larger.

It was flat and moved almost like a manta ray or a bird through the water, flapping its "wings" up and down to propel itself forward. But the head did not have a beak; no, it had a wide, gaping mouth filled with rows of sharp teeth. The monster was gobbling up any straggler sparkfish as if it was completely oblivious to their jolts.

And then its emotionless black eyes noticed me.

It screeched like a hawk and shot forward.

I shook myself out of my trance and turned back toward land. I was going to have to swim faster than I had ever swum before. I could never have outrun it in the middle of the lake, but here I was so close to the shore and it was so big, I just needed to get a little bit further to be safe. . . . I hoped.

Desire. Dedication. Determination. I chanted these three words in my head over and over to keep from completely freaking out. I could do this.

But I couldn't waste time looking back. I could feel that it was right behind me.

It let out another screech—sounding much closer this time—and my blood ran cold. At any moment I expected its jaws to clamp around my leg.

Then I felt it.

Not sharp teeth tearing into my flesh, but solid ground underfoot. I stood, ran through the shallows, and threw myself onto the beach.

Looking back, I could only see the shadow of the creature's body in the shallows and the slight ripple on the surface as it banked and turned to swim back to the deep.

I heaved a dramatic sigh of relief that would have made Tandy proud. In a land where fish could appear and disappear, who knew if that terrifying thing could live out of the water? I thanked my lucky stars that it didn't.

My hand dug into the sandy beach, and something poked my palm. Hoping it wasn't another creature with teeth, I slowly pulled my hand from the sand so as not to startle whatever I was holding.

Light spilled through my fingers, and my palm felt strangely warm. When I opened my hand, I saw the crescent moon shell in my palm.

How did it end up here on the beach, right where I happened to come ashore?

The talk with Mom started replaying in my head. The stuff about Aventurine.

Was this it?

Had I discovered Aventurine in my dreams?

For some reason, I felt totally goofy for a minute, like I was on some kind of reality television show and expected to find camera crews following me, ready to jump out and capture the surprised look on my face when I finally laid eyes on the mystical place my mother had told us stories about all our lives.

Instead, what I saw was a vast lake stretching out toward the horizon and, when I turned around, a thick forest behind me. It was strangely quiet, like a storm was about to break. Except that the sky was shockingly blue and sunny.

Then another thought occurred to me: *Tandy!*

My last memory, before dropping off to sleep, was Tan and me talking in our bedroom. If I was here, where was she?

"Tan!" I called, standing up and walking along the shore.

What do you want, Little LeeLee? Can't you see I'm trying to sleep?

It was Tan's voice. It sounded like it was coming from the trees, so I raced over and peered behind the trunks, trying to find her amongst all the shrubs and leaves. "Tan? Tan, where are you? Can you see me?"

No, doof! My eyes are closed, and it's dark and I'm trying to sleep.

Now that I was standing a little way into the forest, I realized that her voice didn't sound any closer or any further away. It wasn't coming from the forest at all. It almost sounded like . . . like it was coming from . . . the shell? I held the shell closer to my ear, and Tandy's voice came in loud and clear: *Stop bugging me . . . unless you really need me. Call me if you really need me, and I'll be there.*

4

Following the Threads

Whoa.

When we were really little, Tandy and I used to play telephone with empty cans and strings and pretend we could hear voices coming from seashells, but actually hearing her voice through a shell like it was a telephone was *so* cool!

Still, I would rather have had her here with me. It didn't feel right to be in the land that Mom had always told both of us about without her.

Plus, Tandy would know where to go now. She would have some kind of intuition and head off down one of the paths winding through the trees.

That's when I noticed it.

Something in the trees. I stepped into the forest and took a slow turn beneath the arching branches. The deeper I walked into the trees, the better I could see. These were no ordinary leaves. What *was* that hanging, draped from the branches?

Threads.

Gorgeous, luxurious strands of emerald-, silver-, gold-, amethyst-, and opal-colored threads stretched from tree to tree. It didn't matter if the tree was oak or birch or pine. The bright strands stretched off into the distance.

My fingers itched to touch them, but they were too high up in the branches for me to reach. I just knew they'd be the silkiest things I'd ever felt. Scarlet, turquoise, jade . . . so many colors. If Tandy and I ever made bracelets out of these strands, we'd have the most beautiful jewelry around. Way better than anything we'd ever made before. We'd make a killing selling it online.

The amazing thing was—well, besides that there were colorful threads laced through the trees—none of the threads were tangled or knotted. They were all perfectly draped in a line along both sides of a path leading deeper into the woods.

If Tandy were here, she would say this was a sign. Clearly this was the way toward civilization. I gripped the crescent moon shell in my fist and started off down the dirt path.

It was hard to remember to keep an eye out for

trouble. All I wanted to do was gaze up at the threads in the trees. They made me feel like I was following a rainbow to find a pot of gold.

A little way down the path, I noticed that butterflies and birds were perching and flying next to the threads. It took me a second to realize what they were doing, and then I just had to stop and stare with my mouth hanging wide open.

They were fanning the threads with their wings like everything was as normal as sweet potato pie.

Bright yellow butterflies and small sapphire-colored birds flitted around and sat on tangled branches while drying the threads with gusts of air from their wings.

Mom was right; Aventurine was a totally magical place. Suddenly I couldn't wait to see who or what was waiting for me at the end of the path.

I sped up to an easy jog, following the path as it wound deeper and deeper into the forest. Any time I came to a fork in the road, I always followed the threads, trusting my gut that they were leading me the right way.

I came around a bend, and the path widened into a sun-drenched clearing filled with weeping willows and wildflowers. I stopped to take in my surroundings.

Fairies—I could tell by their wings—were grouped around a large loom. These weren't fairy-tale fairies that could be trapped in a bottle like fireflies. No, these fairies were even taller than me and dressed in the most brilliantly colored dresses I'd ever seen. No two fairies wore the same color, and they all had sprays of flowers woven into their hair.

The loom itself was also unusual. It looked like it was made out of crystal and—strangest of all— hummingbirds were acting as the warp, pulling the horizontal threads across the tight vertical ones at lightning speed in aerial maneuvers my eyes couldn't follow.

I thought about contacting Tandy with the shell and describing the scene to her, but she had said that I should only call on her when I really needed her. And coming upon a group of fairies and a magical loom probably didn't qualify as an emergency.

I had been so intent on studying the loom that it took me a moment to realize that the fairies had all turned around and were star- ing at me and whispering amongst themselves.

I thought I heard Songa Lineage mentioned, but I couldn't be sure.

My stomach was starting to weave itself into knots. It's one thing to be staring at fairies. It's quite another to have them staring back at you! I felt like the new girl at school who had to stand up in front of the class and say something about herself.

I waved at them awkwardly, which was totally stupid. I should have just walked over and introduced myself. But it's hard to approach a group of strangers when they're dressed in gorgeous gowns and you're dressed in a purple wet suit.

Across the clearing, a large willow swept aside its branches, and a fairy stepped out into the sunlight. From the way the other fairies turned to look at her, I knew she was their leader right away.

The fairy wore a pale purple dress that shimmered as she moved. Small seed pearls were embroidered around the hem and neckline in an intricate flower pattern. Her brown curls were piled high on her head and cascaded down her back all the way to her knees. And nestled in her curls was a dewdrop crown that shone like diamonds. Like the other fairies, she had flowers—violets—woven into her hair. As she approached, her iridescent blue wings opened and closed like a butterfly's, and the scent of lilacs perfumed the air. I could even see bees buzzing around her lazily—not a fashion choice I would go with!

"Welcome to Aventurine, Lilu," she said, gliding to a stop in front of me and smiling warmly.

"Thank you," I replied, and bobbed into

what I hoped wasn't a complete mess of a curtsy.

"I'm Queen Patchouli of the Willowood Fairies. Please, follow me. You must be curious why you're here, and time is short." She glanced ruefully at the loom. "It's a shame you have come when things are so urgent. I would have loved to discuss weaving with a member of the Songa Lineage. The Willowood Fairies are known for our magical cloth, but your family is legendary for its weaving skills."

I ducked my head so that Queen Patchouli wouldn't see me blush. Did she know that I wasn't as good at weaving as the other women in my family? I hoped I wouldn't disappoint her.

Queen Patchouli led me to the willow tree with its branches pulled back. When we entered, the branches released down like tent flaps closing.

The area was much larger than it appeared from outside. There were a few large rocks and huge mushrooms to the right and an ornately carved desk and chair to the left.

Queen Patchouli rang a glass bell and then gestured for me to sit on a moss-covered rock while she settled onto one of the mushrooms. I thought the seat would be hard, but the moss felt like an overstuffed cushion.

Fairies brought me nectar in a daffodil

cup and a candied water lily cake with some kind of purple frosting that burst with flavors I couldn't even begin to describe—except to say that it was good. Really, really good. I set the crescent moon shell in my lap to free my hands so I could eat more.

Filling my belly with fairy food, I felt that Aventurine had become more real than the waking world, even though so many strange and magical things were happening.

Queen Patchouli waited until I had finished brushing fairy cake crumbs off of my lap. Then she said, "You must have questions about why you are here. First, let me say that you have arrived just in time to begin a very important quest, and unfortunately there isn't a lot of time for explanations. But if you have questions about Aventurine, please ask them now."

With the spotlight on me, I almost didn't know where to begin. There were so many questions I wanted to ask! I bit the inside of my lip. "Am I dreaming? I am, right? I mean, I was in bed, talking to my twin sister, then . . . well, I was underwater. When I wake up, will all this be just a dream?"

Queen Patchouli nodded thoughtfully. "You may be sleeping in your world, but here in Aventurine, you are wide awake and ready to embark on the journey of your life. Do not mistake what takes place here as 'just a dream.' It matters very much how successful you are. However, when you return to your world and wake in your bed, only one night will have passed."

That made sense, I guess. "My mom told me that coming to Aventurine was the start of my training to become a fairy godmother. What does that mean? What do fairy godmothers do?" I asked.

"She was right. You are now a fairy-godmother-in-training. You are gifted with the magic of your Songa Lineage, and I think you will find that your weaving skills will come in handy both here in Aventurine and in the waking world.

"Fairy godmothers are the keepers of the green world and the caretakers of those in need. It is not an easy charge, but those who succeed in their quests and become fairy godmothers join an extraordinary group of strong, magical women. It's a very special thing."

I sat up a little straighter on my moss-covered chair, trying to look worthy of the challenge.

Queen Patchouli's warm green eyes measured me for a second, then she stood and gave me a determined nod. "Come, we have much to do before you must leave."

I stood, gripped the crescent moon shell in my

hand, and followed her to the large desk that I had noticed when we first entered the willow tent. As we neared, I realized the desk was not made of carved wood as I had originally thought.

It was made out of honeycomb! The latticework of the comb made a thick base. The top looked like a sheet of honey had been poured into the comb and then frozen to create a shining amber surface.

The chair was also honeycomb, in some parts thick and in others as thin as my pinkie finger. The seat was woven of long-stemmed wildflowers.

The desk and chair were so fragile-looking and beautiful that when Queen Patchouli motioned for me to sit, I hesitated, afraid I would break the chair.

"Don't worry, Lilu," said Queen Patchouli, noticing my hesitation. "Sometimes beautiful things are not as fragile as they appear."

I gingerly sat and marveled that the chair could hold me. Queen Patchouli was right; it was quite sturdy.

Suddenly the top of the desk began to ripple. Rising out of the golden depths was a large book with a gilded cover. *The Book of Dreams,* I read across its front. Alongside it a crystal jar filled with honey-colored ink rose up as well.

Queen Patchouli handed me a peacock-feather quill. She probably pulled it out of thin air. I had been too busy staring into the desk and wondering what else would float out of its depths to keep an eye on her as well. The desk seemed to be finished now, though, so I turned my attention back to the fairy queen.

"This is *The Book of Dreams,*" said Queen Patchouli. "All fairy-godmothers-in-training write down the one dream that means the most to them. Now it is your turn."

"Every single fairy-godmother-in-training?" I asked.

She nodded.

"That means my mom's dream is in here!"

"Yes." With a flick of her wrist, Queen Patchouli opened the book to my mother's entry.

I gripped the crescent moon shell, realizing that my mother had sat in front of this book when she was my age. It was one thing to hear that she had been here before me; it was quite another to see her familiar handwriting on the page of a magical book.

I don't want to just weave baskets and bracelets anymore. I want to weave words into fabulous stories that move people and change them. I dream of strangers watching my shows and feeling as happy or sad as I felt when I was writing the script and making the film. I just wish I had the right words to say this to my mother without her thinking that I don't appreciate our family's basket-weaving heritage.

—Cassandra

Whoa.

I was beginning to feel like reading this book was a bit like reading someone's diary. Mom had never said anything about having a tough time telling Nan-Nan about wanting to write stories and create documentaries.

It was such a strange feeling. This page held the dream of my mother's younger self. I wished I could shout into the pages and back through the years to let her know that everything would be all right. That she would find a way to tell Nan-Nan and become a success.

A lump rose in my throat.

"Are you ready?" asked Queen Patchouli.

I nodded, and she flicked her wrist again so that the pages fanned to a stop on a fresh tea-colored page.

Penmanship was never really my thing. Tandy was always the one who wrote the thank-you notes to our customers when we filled online orders. I gripped the quill and carefully dipped its tip into the golden ink. For several seconds, my hand hovered over the page.

From the corner of my eye, I saw Queen Patchouli watching me.

I drew a deep breath, exhaled, and wrote my dream as neatly and honestly as I could:

I want my family to be back like we used to be. Like we were supposed to be. Together. Loving and taking care of each other. Everyone is drifting apart. First Mom and Dad. Now Jandy and me. Twins should stick together. My one true dream is having my sister share my world again.

— *Lilu*

I raised my quill from the page and looked up at Queen Patchouli. "And that is your dream?" she asked.

I said yes, and she gave a slight nod. "Very well."

When I looked back at my entry, my jaw dropped. The page was filling in with decorations!

A tight weave was forming around the edge of the page, and a crescent moon shell decorated the top. The bottom looked like two silhouettes with clasped hands were standing at the edge of an ocean with waves coming in. They were united, and I could tell by their hair—my Afro puff and Tandy's relaxed curls— that they were meant to represent Tandy and me. I felt a smile spread across my face like butter on a hot bun.

"Now, if you follow me, I will explain more about your specific quest. And why it is so urgent that you move with haste," said Queen Patchouli. She turned and walked to the center of the tent, where the gnarled willow tree's trunk rose above our heads and split off into arching branches.

When she rested her hand against the trunk, it was as if the entire tree shimmied in response to her touch. The swooping branches tousled like wild hair on a windy day. The willow seemed very glad to see Queen Patchouli.

Her lips moved a bit, but despite my years of developing almost superhuman eavesdropping skills to figure out what was going on with my mom and dad, and then my mom and George, I couldn't hear what she was saying.

I must have been getting used to this whole magic business, because when a crack of green light appeared at the tree's base and sliced its way up the trunk and over to the right, I only jumped a little.

The door formed quickly, and a knot in the tree's bark became a doorknob that Queen Patchouli grasped and pulled open, revealing a flash of bright green that soon faded to black.

I couldn't see anything in the pitch darkness past the doorway in the tree's trunk.

Queen Patchouli turned back to me. "Everything in Aventurine is connected. If you know the proper way to ask, a tree in one area can open a pathway to another. This wise willow has agreed to let us through to the Night Bloomers' Cave, which marks the beginning of the Silven Marsh and your adventure."

With that, she disappeared into the darkness.

I felt silly just standing there in front of the door. Besides, who knew how long the magic would last? Nothing worse than getting left out of your own adventure. Squaring my shoulders, I stepped through the door and into the dark.

5

Through the Night Bloomers' Cave

Have you ever played with Silly Putty?

Well, I can tell you that *being* Silly Putty is not nearly as fun! When I stepped through the door, everything went black, and I felt like a hand had grabbed one edge of me and stretched me out across a big void. It didn't hurt, really, but I felt thin, like I had stopped being a solid person and had become just thoughts in a cloud. Then *SNAP!*—the back of me flung across the void, too, and suddenly I was on the other side.

Queen Patchouli was waiting for me.

We stood in a passageway made of jagged, pale, shimmering quartz. It was spectacular, unlike any place I'd ever seen. Ancient-looking candles lined the walls. I wondered how they stayed lit. Amazing natural stone, polished and gleaming in the dim light, managed to shine with luster. In the distance, I heard birdsong and rushing water.

I followed Queen Patchouli through the passage-way as it narrowed and narrowed until we had to squeeze through an opening, emerging on the other side.

Here, the screech of birds surrounded me, and I could see we had entered a large cave.

This wasn't the kind of cave with bare rock walls and dripping stalactite fangs coming down from the ceiling. It was green and full of life. Gigantic ferns sprouted from all over the place. A grassy clearing, lush and thick with every shade of green imaginable, opened onto a sea of orchids.

Once I stepped clear of the quartz passageway, I was in a waterfall of sunlight on a carpet of grass, the heavy, sweet scent of orchids tingling my nose.

"Where are we?" I asked.

Queen Patchouli looked back. "This is the Night Bloomers' Cave. The ceiling is covered in tiny cave flowers that bloom at night and glow with this magical sunlight. All of the plants and animals here rely on the light to survive," she said with a smile.

So that means while this part of the world is experiencing nighttime, Willowood is experiencing daytime, I thought. I wondered if that meant that traveling through the willow had taken me all day in the blink of an eye or if I'd just traveled clear around to the other side of Aventurine. Just thinking about it made my head hurt!

The queen led me through a maze of ferns, moss, and birds—there were so many here. Glossy ibises, tall and thin; great blue herons, alert and noble. But the most amazing of all the birds were . . .

The cranes. They were larger than in the waking world, and their bright feathers shimmered in the night bloomers' light.

I couldn't help myself. "Whooping cranes? You have endangered whooping cranes here, too?"

Queen Patchouli stopped by two tall, majestic cranes standing at the edge of an underground river.

The birds both turned and looked at me at the same time.

I know it sounds ridiculous, but they were looking right at me, right into my eyes. And it was like, well, like I could almost feel what they were thinking. They seemed sad, but maybe hopeful, too.

Mom and Dad were both whooping crane enthusiasts. Hmm . . . no wonder I was such a mess. Any time a girl can make a statement like her parents are "whooping crane enthusiasts," well, you've got to expect her to be a little daffy, right?

Anyway, I remembered a lot from all the times Tan and I worked with both of them to spread awareness about the dwindling whooping crane population. There are less than five hundred whooping cranes left in the world. All kinds of programs exist with people trying different ways to rebuild their populations and get them to reproduce, but Mom says it's tough.

"Lilu," said Queen Patchouli, "I know that in your world, you are being challenged with a great many changes."

I bit the corner of my lip but remained silent. She beckoned for me to take a seat beside her on a quartz bench cut into the cavern's side.

When I sat, she took my hand and squeezed my fingers. Then she drew a deep breath and began to explain the true reason I had been called there. "Aventurine is going through change as well. A storm is coming. Worse than a hurricane, because it has magic at its root. The Tangerine Tide, we call it, which is a pretty name for something that has the power to cause some very ugly damage.

"You see, a lot of magic is used in Aventurine, and bits of it are often left over in the air after spells have been cast. Those bits float around, sometimes helping plants and animals grow into healthy beings, but every hundred years or so enough of the magic collects in the clouds to churn into a storm. The storm then feeds on itself, growing bigger and bigger until it blows through an area with terrible force." Queen Patchouli shuddered. "When that happens, it sucks up all the water in the area, leaving behind a sticky orange mess—a tangerine tide of destruction."

This sounded really bad. Lots of wind and rain could be devastating to animal communities. I wondered how the birds of the marsh would prepare. Or if they would survive.

"There isn't a lot of time. The Tangerine Tide moves quickly. We've already had the storm that blows through as a warning of its arrival. It was terrible, and besides causing some destruction to the marsh, which is bad enough, it separated these two whooping cranes, Zeus and Zandria, from one of their eggs. An egg that will hatch into a baby boy crane soon," said Queen Patchouli.

In the waking world, whooping cranes usually have two eggs and then choose to raise only one of the eggs. Here, they must be able to keep both.

I turned to look at the stately whooping crane parents. In a tuft of saw grass and twigs I spotted a single, perfect egg.

Now I realized why the birds looked so sad. They had lost a baby!

"You will need to travel to the Castle on Stilts. That is where Queen Alaina of the Dragonfly Fairies has kept the egg since the storm blew it onto her land. If you can reach her in time and return with the egg before the Tangerine Tide reaches the marshlands, you will have a chance to reunite it with its family."

When my eyes practically bugged out of my head, Queen Patchouli gave me a stern look. "Becoming a fairy godmother relies on a girl's ability to use her special gifts—her powers—in a way that makes her stronger as well as strengthens those around her. Not everyone who is given a challenge is able to fulfill that promise."

This was way more intense than making sure I had the right body alignment for a rip entry in my springboard dive. If my dive was off, I'd just wind up with a lousy score. But this?

"What if . . . I mean, really. I might fail. Then Zeus and Zandria will lose their child because of me! It would be all my fault."

The idea made me shiver. Near the water's edge, where a thin ribbon of foam pushed back and forth across the lip of grass, the whooping cranes peered at me with watchful eyes. Waiting.

"If you go on this journey and give it your all, Zeus and Zandria will understand that you tried."

"But this was probably their only chance to, you know, um . . ." This was embarrassing stuff to talk about with a queen.

"Reproduce." Queen Patchouli squeezed my fingers again as she said the word. I felt my face and ears get so warm I thought I was at a bonfire—and *I* was the marshmallow getting toasted!

I blew out a long sigh. "I know a lot about their behaviors. I know they're endangered. And I know that people with a lot more experience than me have tried a lot of different ways to help them migrate and, um, you know, reproduce and all. It's really tough. That's one of the main reasons why they're so rare."

"Indeed. But what you have is something that many others do not—you have a strong bond with earth, air, fire, and water. Your ancestral heritage as part of the Songa Lineage connects you to the elements and provides you with everything you need."

"But I don't think—" I started to protest.

"No one can tell you how your journey will end, but that isn't the point. The only thing that matters is the adventure that lies ahead and how or if you will choose to proceed."

But it wasn't just a challenge or a dare. It was more.

Queen Patchouli had this way of looking at me. It was like looking into a combination of strong-woman eyes—Mom, Nan-Nan, Coach Regina. Just like the other women in my life who pushed me to push myself, Queen Patchouli's gaze penetrated me and made me feel like no matter what happened, she had faith in me. Slowly, I began to nod.

Suddenly two really big blue and green dragonflies zipped across my face and circled Queen Patchouli's head.

I swatted at them, but she just laughed.

"Stop it, you two. It's time for you to meet Lilu," she said.

The dragonflies hovered in the air before us. They sizzled with a zapping sound, sort of like what those electric bug zappers on Nan-Nan's back porch sounded like. The dragonflies expanded until they were the size of a model airplane, then the size of a large kite.

I shrank back in my seat, not quite sure how big these bugs were planning on growing!

At that moment, they began to sparkle and glow. And all of a sudden, I was staring at two twin fairy girls the same size as me!

Queen Patchouli stood, and I followed her lead.

"Lilu, I'm pleased to introduce you to Hanna and Jo. They are Dragonfly Fairies and guides on your quest. They will show you the way to Queen Alaina's Castle on Stilts."

"Hello," I said. I felt more nervous meeting these girls than I had been when I met Queen Patchouli.

"Hi! Nice to meet you, Lilu," said Hanna with a friendly wave.

"Hi," said Jo, giving me a brief nod.

The twin fairies had skin the color of dark coffee and ink-black hair in the thinnest braids I'd ever seen, which hung to their calves. Their dragonfly wings had transformed into shimmering pearl-colored fairy wings, longer and thinner than Queen Patchouli's.

The only noticeable difference between the two was their startling eyes. Hanna's were an electric green, while Jo's were a shockingly bright shade of blue.

I'd never seen anyone with eyes that color, but I gave a mental shrug—they were magical fairy creatures after all!

Magical fairy creatures with a seriously hot sense of style.

Hanna was wearing a high-waisted black skirt

that seemed to be made out of beetle shells—or maybe dragonfly skins?—knit together. Every time she moved, her skirt shone with a blue-black glow like it was sewn from tiny sequins. Her shirt was the same vivid green as her eyes and seemed to be made of silk, though it was probably made out of unicorn hair or something. Her shoes were the same black ballet flats that I'd noticed on all of the fairies so far. But these had black ribbons that laced around her ankles and tied in a delicate bow in the back.

Jo wore what looked like buttery-soft black leather leggings with a long black tunic. The tunic was cinched around her waist with a wide belt the same color as her blue eyes. The weave of her belt was extraordinarily complicated, with bright beads flashing throughout.

Man, was I sick of this purple wet suit!

"I'll bet you'd like to change into something more appropriate for your journey," said Queen Patchouli.

"Yes!" I said, nodding enthusiastically. "That would be great. But I don't have any other clothes here."

"Don't worry about that," said Hanna. "Patchouli's got you covered."

"It's true. Every fairy-godmother-in-training gets her own special wardrobe. It's part of your journey," said Queen Patchouli.

Queen Patchouli walked to the river's edge and moved her left hand like she was stirring a pot. The water froze and then swirled, mimicking her hand motion, until it rose up to create a cylinder of moving water right in the river!

"You'll find everything you need in there. Just step through," said Queen Patchouli.

It was much easier to step through a wall of moving water than into a pitch-black doorway in a willow tree's trunk. An icy chill washed over me as I walked into the impromptu dressing room, but I stayed dry and the dark rippling water provided complete privacy.

A large wardrobe carved out of ice stood in front of me. It was pretty plain except for a crescent moon carved into the top, which reminded me of the crescent moon shell I was still clutching. I decided to find a bag for it in this wardrobe.

When I opened the wardrobe, I couldn't help letting out a little shriek of excitement. I had officially entered a dreamworld of clothes! All this time I had been imagining a movie-of-the-week version of my family; well, now I just wanted to do a movie montage of trying on outfits!

My stomach clenched. Tan should have been there to try on these clothes with me. We would have had so much fun! Just like our trips to the mall when we both selected one ridiculous outfit that the other girl had to try on. The trips always ended with laughing fits in front of the mirror.

I sighed and studied the options. I didn't want to take too long since Queen Patchouli had said the storm was moving fast.

The wardrobe was packed with clothes, and mirrors hung on the inside of each door. There were elaborate dresses and flowing skirts of materials so soft and silky they might as well have been made out of clouds. Brightly patterned blouses and crocheted tops of all shades hung to the left of the dresses and skirts.

On my right, every type of pants imaginable, from patched jeans and leggings to linen shorts, hung next to scarves and bags. Underneath I found a drawer filled with shoes, and again every style was represented, from completely impractical sky-high heels to equally ridiculous pink rain boots.

I shucked off my wet suit and water shoes—finally!—and quickly tried on a dress with crocheted straps and detailing. It was a beautiful crisp white. But then I thought about the camping trips my family used to go on. There was no way white was going to fly, and a dress probably wasn't all that realistic, either.

Next I pulled out a silky pink tank top as soft as flower petals. It would be easy to move in. Nearby, there was a creamy crocheted shrug to layer over the tank top.

A pair of pants in a berry-red color caught my eye. They were fitted cargo capris with loads of pockets—perfect for storing my crescent moon shell!

I tried on the silky top, crocheted shrug, and comfy pants and spun in front of the mirrors. Not too shabby!

In the drawer of shoes I found gold-colored woven sandals. When I slipped them on, they wove themselves to my feet! These were definitely not going to need to be broken in.

I checked myself in the mirrors again but still felt like something was missing. Rummaging through drawers, I came up with a few much-needed accessories: lots of braided and beaded bracelets and a red headband to push back my naturally springy curls into a cute Afro puff. The bright berry color popped against my dark brown hair.

I was ready.

I stepped back through the water to the small group waiting at the river's edge.

Hanna whistled appreciatively as I did a little twirl in my new outfit. "I love that shrug," she said.

71

"Lilu," said Queen Patchouli, "do you have your crescent moon shell?"

I unzipped my pants pocket and handed the shell to her.

She took a single strand of saw grass from the brush at the river's edge and wound it around her wrist. The hearty grass began to change, softening until it turned into a sparkling silver ribbon. Then Queen Patchouli used the ribbon to pierce a single hole through the crescent moon shell and draped it around my neck.

I felt my cheeks redden. It was like being awarded my diving medal all over again.

"Touch the crescent," she said. I hesitated, but she insisted. "Go on."

So I did.

Cucimita. Good luck, my beautiful sister.

It was Tandy. I could still hear her loud and clear without holding the shell to my ear.

"Although you are here and she is not quite here, if you need your sister, touch the necklace. She will always be with you."

Next, Zandria brought over beautiful white and yellow water lilies. She dropped them gently into Queen Patchouli's outstretched hands.

Queen Patchouli intertwined their stems, which appeared to be dripping wet, then stuck them in my hair behind my ear. I cringed, waiting for the water to trickle into my blouse, but . . . no trickle.

"They're so beautiful. But they're water flowers. They'll die quickly, won't they?"

Queen Patchouli smiled. "They are very special. The lilies are all part of a bigger plan. Use them when you need them most, but their fragrance and beauty are yours forever."

She told me that Hanna and Jo were my special gifts as well. "They will be your fairy guides. Just remember, *you* are the leader and this is your mission."

Hanna and Jo both nodded their agreement.

Then Queen Patchouli gave me a small item. Wood. With carvings.

"A totem?" I asked.

She nodded. "You should find this totem useful on your journey."

I studied the dark

wood engravings and saw the roaring head of a lion merging with the body of a crocodile.

"But . . . how?" I said, bewildered. How could any of these things help me speed past a magical hurricane, rescue a lost crane egg, and return it in time to hatch with its twin?

"Queen Patchouli, I don't under—" I had been looking down, staring at the totem. When I looked up, Queen Patchouli was gone.

6

The Ba-dum Boat

I did a quick spin. "Where—"

But I didn't have a chance to finish my question. Jo and Hanna began tugging me along the riverbank. They pulled me around a bend, and the lush ferns parted to reveal the cave's opening and the edge of the Silven Marsh.

As bright as the cave had been, the marsh was bathed in darkness. A fat silver moon sat high in the star-speckled sky, and night creatures sang their songs.

"You have everything you need. Everything Queen Patchouli can give you. The rest is up to you," Jo said.

"And we're here to help you, too, of course," said Hanna.

I was still too stunned to speak. The twin fairies

half pushed, half tugged me up to the marsh's edge, where a long boat was tied. I climbed aboard after Hanna, as Jo unhooked the lines from the shore and pushed the boat off.

"Wow," I said, turning in a circle and taking it all in. "This is *not* your average boat!"

The wooden craft had a flat bottom with decorative veins of silver swirling through it as though to represent the wind or waves. The bow had five ruby-red drums arranged in a semicircle. The four to the right were all the same size and had an hourglass shape that made me feel like I'd seen them before, though I couldn't quite place them. The drum to the left was much smaller — a miniversion of the others.

The sides of the boat rose up to hip level and had pillows, blankets, and boxes — that I assumed contained supplies — all neatly arranged and tied down with strong cords. We seemed to be well stocked for our adventure.

As Jo flitted aboard — how cool would it be to have wings? — I moved to the stern to investigate the strange contraption sticking up where a fan would be if this were a normal marsh airboat. A wooden capital *T* stood up and out of the deck. The top of the T had six chimes on either side — twelve total. They had a pearly sheen and stayed unnaturally still despite the breeze stirring the air and the general rocking of the boat.

I reached out to flick one of the chimes, just to see what would happen.

"I wouldn't do that if I were you," said Jo, stopping my hand.

"Oh, let her experiment," said Hanna.

"And have her tip us over? Bad idea. Really bad. This mission must be a success. Don't risk everything in the first five minutes, Hanna."

"Um, guys, I'm standing right here," I said, giving a little wave. Their sisterly bickering made me feel like an outsider. I touched the crescent moon shell and felt a wave of now-familiar longing for Tan wash over me.

"Sorry, Lilu," said Hanna, sticking her tongue out at her sister. "Jo acts like she has a rip in her wing over the stupidest stuff. Have you ever been in a ba-dum boat before?"

"No, I've never been in *anything* like this. Where's the motor? Why are there drums and chimes?" I asked.

Hanna pulled out two pillows from the starboard side and settled gracefully onto one in front of the drums. She flicked her long braids so that they spread out behind her and then patted the pillow beside her. "Sit down and find out. You're in for the ride of your life!" She laughed.

I plunked myself down onto the pillow and watched as Hanna began tapping out a slow, steady beat on the drums. The boat shuddered and then sprang to life. I could feel it waking up around me, as though Hanna were tapping out its heartbeat and raising it from the dead. I leaned my head over the side of the boat and gasped. The boat was two feet off the water! We were hovering in the air.

"Ready, Jo?" Hanna called back over her shoulder.

"Ready!"

Hanna gave me a wink. "Here we go!" she sang out.

She beat the drums in a stronger, faster rhythm. The boat responded to the new beat and glided forward across the moonlit marsh.

A memory tickled the back of my brain. What was that sound?

The rhythm was so steady, peaceful. The calm before the storm.

Except inside me, a storm was already raging. How was I going to do this without Tandy by my side? What kinds of creatures were living out here in this marsh? The whole mission seemed so strange. So impossible.

Clasping the seashell, I shut my eyes to the wind. My heart thumped to the rhythm of the mysterious beat. *Tandy! Tandy! Costago! Costago!*

Chill, Lilu. Why do you need my help?

She sounded so far away. I didn't just want her voice in my ear. I needed her with me. *Tan! I can't even begin to tell you all that is going on, but right now I'm flying through a dark marsh on some sort of magical airboat—*

She yawned. YAWNED! I was possibly about to encounter the Creature from the Black Lagoon or Swamp Thing or worse, and my impending death was boring my sister.

Hanna noticed me touching the crescent moon shell. She sighed and beat faster on the drums.

I'm not sure why Hanna was upset with me. Isn't it normal for twins to want to consult each other? Be there for each other? Her sister was here, and mine was in another world—who was she to judge? She wasn't looking, so I quickly stuck my tongue out at her, just to feel better.

Little LeeLee, listen, I'm really trying to get some rest. You'll be fine. Just turn down the music.

What music?

Stop messing with me, Lilu. I can hear it. That schnick-schnick-schnick *in the background. It's the djembe drums. Same as Nan-Nan taught us. Well, tried to teach us. You were always too embarrassed to play. Anyway, she said the tune was passed down from her great-grandmama so-and-so. Turn that off and concentrate. You'll be fine. Just fine . . .*

Before she could say anything else, I'd lost the connection. I sure hoped this seashell would start to get better service than the el cheapo cell phones Mom had bought us.

Then what Tandy had said clicked. That's where I'd heard it before!

The familiar rhythm powering the boat was the same beat our grandmother taught us long ago. I blew out a long sigh and let the tense muscles in my neck, back, and legs relax.

An image fluttered into my head, one I hadn't thought of in years. The four of us—Nan-Nan, Mom, Aunt Mary, and Tandy—sitting together on Nan-Nan's back porch. We're talking and laughing, and Nan-Nan is about to begin a story. Nan-Nan, Mom, and Aunt Mary used to tell us these really cool folk-tales that dated back to our ancestors in Africa. They talked about the rhythm of life and our unique connection with the elements. Nan-Nan used to say, "Everyone has a road to walk in this life. The trick, my babies, is knowing when to stay on the road and knowing when to make a new one."

And she would always sing us this one song, while Mom and Aunt Mary played the djembes. Tan and I would sit on the floor, tapping our toes and weaving jewelry to the beat.

The Weaver's Song

Everything is one
Never come undone
Take a bit of moonlight
Weave it with the sun
Steal the fire's flame
Tie the waves upon
Spin it into cloth
Wear it like a cloak
Always be the water
Always be the warmth
Everything is one
Never come undone
Everything is one
Never come undone

Nan-Nan had a way of making everything sound so simple — black and white. Except sometimes things you thought were one *do* come undone.

As I settled on my pillow and watched the ba-dum boat wind its way through the moonlight-tipped marsh, I wondered about the road we were traveling. Were we heading in the right direction? Would I know what to do when we got there?

Speaking of heading in the right direction, I wondered how Hanna was steering this thing. That's when it occurred to me to look back at Jo.

Jo was meticulously tapping on the chimes at the stern of the boat. She had the same concentrated look on her face as the ringers in the handbell choir at my church — like she wouldn't see me if I were in front of her; she would only see the music and the knowledge of when to ring her bell.

Now that I was watching her, I could hear the light chiming underneath Hanna's beat on the drums. I studied Jo's movements and felt the effect of them on the boat.

Jo was steering the boat with music!

Whenever she tapped a higher note, the craft adjusted its route to the left, and whenever she struck a lower note, the craft veered to the right. So cool! I could understand now why she didn't want me messing with the chimes earlier. It clearly took a lot of skill to strike the right note for the boat to swerve and avoid hitting clumps of reed grass and cattails as we zipped over the marsh.

If Hanna was playing the heartbeat that fueled the boat's motor, then Jo was playing the thoughts that directed the boat's rudder.

"This is the coolest boat ever," I said to myself.

Hanna heard me. "I've never been on any kind of boat except this. Dragonfly Fairies use these all the time when we're covering long distances across the marsh," she said.

"Does flying tire your wings out?" I asked. I was curious about fairies in general. Queen Patchouli hadn't been the type who I could ask a whole lot of personal questions, but Hanna seemed friendly and open.

"In fairy form, we can't go very far at all. The Kib and Willowood Fairies are way better fliers than us, and I've heard the Kalistonia Fairies are so good they can dance on the wind. But I've never been to the mountains, so I can't say for sure if that's exaggerated fairy lore or the truth." Hanna tapped the smallest drum to the left and then stopped drumming completely.

I thought we would screech to a halt, but the beat continued on without her needing to drum. "Is that like autopilot or something?" I said, pointing to the small djembe.

"I don't know what autopilot is," said Hanna. "This just keeps the boat moving at the same speed without me having to wear out my hands beating on these drums the whole way.

"Anyway, so in dragonfly form we can fly for miles and miles. It's the *best* way to fly. But you can't carry anything heavier than a dewdrop when you're a dragonfly. You would be *way* too heavy. Even the egg we need to get would be too heavy. So the ba-dum boat is the next best way to travel. It's pretty useful when you're traveling with baggage." She shot me an apologetic look. "Um, not that we think you're baggage or anything. You're a fairy-godmother-in-training, which is a pretty big deal around here. It's, like, a huge honor to help you on this mission, and Jo and I aren't going to screw it up."

"Thanks," I said. "I wasn't insulted, and you and Jo have been really good guides already."

"Really?" Hanna beamed at me. She turned around and shouted, "Hey, Jo, Lilu says we're doing a good job! Nice, huh?"

"Yeah, but we haven't even done anything yet,

Hanna. If you want her to keep thinking that way, maybe you should pay attention. The black swamp area is coming up. We should slow down."

What a wet blanket.

Hanna tapped the djembe to the left and then steadily tapped out a slower rhythm. The ba-dum boat slowed to a crawl.

I hate to admit it, but I hadn't noticed the dark crop of trees ahead. It was probably good that Jo had pointed it out when she did. But would it have killed her to use a friendlier tone?

We slid in amongst the cypresses and followed a slim trail of water that twisted and turned and wound its way deeper and deeper into the trees.

"It's getting too dark out here. We should stop for the night," called Jo.

I wasn't scared of the dark like Tan, but something about this place gave me the chills. Our boat's music reverberated off the trees and echoed around us. Any predator within a mile had to know we were here. Better to get back out into the open, right?

"Let's keep going till we're out of the trees," I said. "Hanna, can you go a little faster? Get us out of here?"

I knew I was being irrational, but I couldn't shake the feeling we were being watched.

Hanna shrugged. "Sure, I'm always game for

more speed," she said. "You're the boss."

"Lilu," said Jo, "I don't think this is smart. We can't see well in here. Let's wait till morning. . . ."

Hanna picked up the tempo and drowned out Jo's protests.

The ba-dum boat gathered speed, and I could hear Jo frantically ringing the chimes—low, low, high, low, high—to keep us out of the trees. A branch on the left scraped along the side and she overcorrected, causing us to bump into a trunk on the right.

It jarred me, and suddenly I was afraid of the speed. Afraid we were losing control. Things would be a whole lot worse if we hit something and damaged the boat. Then we would be stuck out here when the Tangerine Tide blew through, and that would mean big trouble. Nan-Nan almost lost her house the last time a hurricane hit Charleston. Plus, Zeus and Zandria were counting on me.

"Gross, Lilu," groaned Hanna. "We're all scared, but that's no reason to fart."

"What? I did *not* fart," I said. "I don't even smell anything."

The trees were thinning, and I could catch glimpses of the marshlands stretching out in the distance past the next clump of trees. We had almost broken free! Now was *not* the time to make fart jokes.

"Ugh, what did you eat?" Hanna started gagging. "It's not fair. I can't plug my nose when I'm drumming!"

"I told you, it's not me. I don't smell anything!" I said. I turned to look at Jo. "Jo, back me up—"

Jo was lying on her side, completely knocked out!

I raced over to her and started shaking her. "Jo! Jo! Wake up!"

She didn't move.

I heard a thump, and the drumming stopped. Hanna was slumped over the drums. What was going on?

I grabbed my crescent moon shell, but explaining everything to Tan would take time, and the boat was still careening forward. We were going to collide with the last outcrop of trees.

I found the mallet for the chimes in Jo's hand and took it from her stiff fingers. Desperately, I struck the highest note.

The boat veered to the left, but not far enough. We were only a yard away now.

I struck again—hard.

The note hung in the air and the boat took a sharper turn, throwing all of us to the right.

I waited for the impact. Expecting to hear

crunching wood and to be tossed forward.

Nothing.

The ba-dum boat slid to a halt about ten feet from the last clump of trees.

I let out a cheer. But it sounded hollow without Jo and Hanna joining in. What happened? Was there some kind of poison gas?

I felt Jo's neck and found the thrump of her heartbeat, but her breathing was shallow. I crawled up to Hanna and checked her. Same thing.

If it was some kind of gas, how come I wasn't affected, too? All I could smell was the pleasant scent of the water lilies behind my ear.

The water lilies! Had they protected me from the gas?

I took them from behind my ear and held them under Hanna's nose.

That's when the stench hit me. Rotting garbage, raw sewage, vomit, and used baby diapers rolled up into a compost heap would smell like a fresh breeze in comparison. I bowled over and gasped, trying to cover my nose and keep from puking.

Out of the corner of my eye, I could see that the flowers were working— Hanna's eyes began to flutter open. "Mar-marsh frogs." She coughed.

"They're coming." She collapsed in a fit of coughing.

I couldn't understand what she meant. My mind was getting foggy. I could feel my arms getting heavy. Frogs? Why would Hanna sound so afraid of frogs? Frogs don't smell. Do they?

Didn't matter; I needed to take a nap. If I was sleeping, I wouldn't smell anymore.

Suddenly the flowers were back behind my ear.

In my delirious state, I turned to Hanna and thought I could see the lilies' perfume trailing from her face to mine. I waved my hand at the purple streak in the air. It felt like ribbons of silk.

I concentrated and grasped the ribbons. They felt solid now, but slippery. Slowly, carefully, I pulled and pulled on the ribbons in the air. I had an idea, but I would need longer ribbons of perfume for it to work.

When I had a pile of ribbon on the deck, I heard something coming from the trees.

Plop. Plop, plop.

Marsh frogs? I almost turned to look, but the ribbons began to fade when my attention wandered.

I shoved away my fear and calmed my shaking hands. Nothing had changed except that I needed to act faster now.

I imagined the tight weave of surgical masks and began to work, quickly creating a mask big enough to cover Hanna's nose and mouth. The fragrant ribbon fought me, trying to curl or drift out of my grasp, but I strengthened my will and my hold on the strands and wove them even tighter. Soon I bit off one complete scent mask and fit it over Hanna's ears.

The waters around the boat were beginning to ripple.

The second mask was easier than the first, despite my tremors. Then I heard thumps on the bottom of the boat. Something—or some *things*—was jumping out of the water, trying to get into the boat, which was still hovering a foot or two above the water.

I tied off the final knot on the second mask as Hanna began to sit up. I scrambled over to Jo and fit the mask over her nose and mouth. She had been out for so long. I was worried.

The thumping sounded like hard rain pounding on the bottom of the boat. One reddish-brown frog cleared the side and landed by my leg.

"Don't let it touch you!" screamed Hanna.

I grabbed the mallet again and swatted the frog off the boat.

Hanna began pounding a rapid beat on the drums, and we blasted off.

7

A Face in the Trees

I dragged Jo—still motionless—off to the right of the boat and took up position to steer. Luckily the path was wide. It was not hard to adjust our flight path as we escaped.

The boat shot across moon-glossy patches of water, in and out of circles of shadows. Behind us, the trees faded into the distance. To my right, Jo stirred, and I heaved a sigh of relief.

After we'd traveled for some time, Hanna slowed the boat to a gentle stop. She immediately rushed back to her twin. "Jo, Jo, how are you feeling?" she asked softly.

"Mmm, better," mumbled Jo. She was sitting up now, and her eyes were clearing. "What happened?"

"Yeah, what happened?" I echoed.

"Marsh frogs. They're natural predators of

Dragonfly Fairies. But they can kill humans, too. They release an awful smell to knock out their prey, and then they . . . well, their skin is poisonous. First they make it so you can't move, and then the whole pack of them eats you," Hanna said.

"That's awful," I said.

"Queen Patchouli must have foreseen us needing protection. She wisely gave you those lilies to combat the sleeping gas," said Jo, the color returning to her face.

"Smart move, weaving masks out of the perfume, Lilu," said Hanna. "You saved us."

"Thank you, Lilu," said Jo.

She reached out a hand to me, and I pulled her onto her feet. I could tell she wanted to say more, but I cut her off. "You should thank Hanna. I was almost passed out when she pushed the flowers back behind my ear. She sacrificed herself," I said.

"Well, you're the fairy-godmother-in-training. Queen Patchouli gave the flowers to *you*—not Jo or me—because you are the best suited to use them, what with your being from the Songa Lineage and all."

"What do you mean?" I asked.

"Everyone knows the members of the Songa Lineage can weave anything they desire. I've never fully believed it, but I'd be a fool to doubt it now. I'm still wearing a mask you wove out of thin air," marveled Hanna.

She pulled off her mask and studied it. Jo did the same.

"Solid weave," said Jo.

I felt a glow of pride warm my chest and melt the fear that had lodged there when I first saw Jo crumpled under the chimes. In the waking world, I never would have been able to weave a mask so tightly. I could barely weave a basket in the time it took Tandy to weave three.

"It's starting," Hanna said.

Her voice nudged me out of my thoughts. "What's starting?"

"The rain," said Jo, pointing to the dots speckling the deck. "We're going to need to find a place to stop for a while."

"Just until the rain passes. Don't worry. It's not the hurricane. Not yet," said Hanna. "We only need to camp out for a little bit."

Oh, great. What other dangers lurked out here in the marsh? My fingers inched toward the necklace.

Jo caught my hand. "You don't need her," she said.

I reluctantly let my hand drop.

"C'mon," said Hanna. "Let's get moving. We're a

bit off course now, but I think there's an island not too far away. Jo, you know the one?"

Jo nodded and took up her place at the chimes. I sat back down next to Hanna at the djembe drums. It was almost as if nothing had happened; except that a lot *had* happened, and now we were all knit together somehow. I could feel it. Saving each other's lives had bound us together.

Soft, steady beads of rain continued to fall, but we didn't get any wetter. Thin reeds of saw grass emerged from the sides of the boat and wove shimmering silver threads to form a protective canopy over us.

Jo quickly steered us to the island. When we arrived, Hanna tapped out a distinct rhythm that lowered the ba-dum boat back onto the water. Then she flew out with the lines and tied us to some mangrove trees.

Jo took a box from the boat and flew out as well, but then turned to help me down.

My feet were unsteady on the solid ground at first after being on the boat all night. But soon I was helping to set up camp. The boat was as well stocked as I had imagined, so we quickly started a fire and put our tents up and our bedding down.

Orange and red sparks sputtered against pieces of bark. Funny. Before I went to bed last night, the idea of sitting around a campfire built by fairies might have seemed strange. Now I was wondering, *Hey, why haven't I done this sort of thing before?*

Hanna broke open a large pod that provided fresh water, which she poured into a pot. Jo, meanwhile, chopped up strange-looking plants that I assumed were similar to vegetables back home. They both flitted around the campfire, tasting dishes and adding ingredients here and there. They worked like one person split in two. It would have been eerie if I wasn't a twin myself. I knew how well Tandy and I could work together.

"Is there anything I can do to help?" I offered.

"Yeah," said Hanna, "you can weave up a bowl for me. It looks like we only have two sets of dishes here."

"That's weird. Queen Patchouli must've only been expecting two of us to travel or something," I said.

Hanna and Jo shared a strange look.

"Dinner's almost ready, Lilu. Why don't you get started on your bowl?" said Jo.

I went over to the reeds and trimmed off a bunch of strong grasses. Hanna touched them briefly. "Now they're clean," she said.

I sat by the fire and began to work, hopeful that my skill at weaving the perfumed masks would carry over. But, as usual, I was all thumbs. The grasses struggled against me, and focusing my attention on them didn't help like it had with the ribbons of fragrance. It seemed that working with tangible materials was still too hard for me.

Eventually, I had completed a lopsided bowl. Even in the dim firelight, I felt myself blush with embarrassment.

Jo dished me out a portion of delicious-smelling vegetable stew.

"I . . . I'm not that talented with making baskets and things. Not like my mom and sister, or any of my other female relatives. Sorry," I said, and sighed. I hated not being good at something.

"No need to apologize, Lilu," said Jo. "You proved your weaving skills today when it really mattered."

Hanna nodded. "Yeah, don't stress about it."

We began talking about the Songa Lineage. Jo said that their ancestry had a rich lineage of heroes, too. "When you grow up hearing the tales of your ancestors, it fills you with a sense of anticipation, you know?" she said. "How can you not wonder what lies ahead and where your life and adventures will lead?"

I nodded. Then I told them about Nan-Nan. "She used to tell my sister and me these wild stories that had been passed down from generation to generation. Tandy loved acting out the stories, and Nan-Nan would act them out with her. . . ." I let my voice trail off and sat in silence, staring into the fire.

The memory tugged at my mind like a poorly trained puppy on a leash. As plain as day I could see it—Tan and me at Nan-Nan's house, listening to her stories in the kitchen, helping her coax delicate green peas from their pods.

Tandy loved all those old stories. She'd break into some made-up song and dance and act out the whole thing. We'd beat on every pan in the kitchen like they were djembes. I hadn't thought about that in a long time. Tan had always acted. Why had I convinced myself that her love of it was new?

"Can you believe it?" asked Jo. "She's sleeping! We're on a very important mission and she's taking a nap."

The fire was dying out, but lightning bugs flickered like candles in the woods. At first I thought Jo was talking about Tandy, who was home in bed, probably dead asleep. Then I followed her eyes over to her sister. Hanna was lying curled up with her drumming pillow and a blanket.

"I guess she was tired," I said.

Now it was Jo's turn for a big sigh. "Nothing bothers her. Not ever. Hanna is just at peace all the time. Me? I worry about every little detail."

Even as she spoke, she had begun checking the wood to make sure the fire would burn out. I'd done some scouting when I was a kid so I knew the routine.

"It's important for us to help you through this. Very important. So you shouldn't feel like you're in this alone," said Jo.

"I'm never alone. I've got my sister!" I reached for the shell, closed my fingers around it. Then I felt guilty. Jo was opening up, and I was pushing her away.

I said, "Don't get me wrong. I appreciate everything you and Hanna are doing. It's just, well, with Tan and me, I always know that she's looking out for me. You're a twin. You know how it is. You don't have to think twice about it. The other person's just always there."

The rain had stopped. I leaned out from under the tent. A thin, wispy, gray-bearded cloud drifted past the full white moon. Orange goop tinged a nearby puddle—a reminder that we didn't have much time.

Jo looked at me sadly. "You can't always depend on another person to be there, Lilu. Sometimes all you have is yourself," she said.

She looked over at her sister. "Well, maybe Hanna doesn't have a terrible idea. We're all exhausted. A few hours' sleep might be what we need."

I opened my mouth to respond and yawned instead.

"That settles it," said Jo. "Let's get some sleep. Good night, Lilu."

"Good night," I said.

As a red-tinged sun spilled its bloody glow over the edge of the marsh, I woke to a stick digging painfully into my leg. I felt around and pulled out of my pocket the wooden totem Queen Patchouli had given me. In the morning light, the lion appeared to be growling at me, like it was mad that I had slept.

Noticing my movements, Jo hurried over. "We have to go now, Lilu," she said.

I rose and stretched. The fire was banked, and the camp had been completely broken down except for the tent and my pillow and blanket.

"You guys should have woken me up earlier," I said.

"We thought you deserved a bit more sleep. That magic you did yesterday probably took a lot out of you," said Jo.

Magic? It hadn't occurred to me that I had been doing magic when I weaved the masks. I guess it made sense, though; people normally can't weave solid things out of the elements. Magic must've been involved. The thought that I could have it in me was exciting and unsettling. What did it mean for my future? Would I be able to weave magic in the waking world? That would be amazing!

I packed up my stuff and loaded it onto the ba-dum boat.

"Red sky in morning, sailor take warning," said Jo.

We all glanced at the red puffy clouds piling up in the distance. This was not a good sign.

Hanna handed each of us a thick slice of spongy spice cake and passed around a water pod.

Refreshed, we took up our positions and quickly set off. It amazed me how familiar I was already with the rhythm of the s and the tinkling of the chimes.

Despite the urgency of our mission, the morning was pretty dull. We flew as fast as we safely could and didn't come upon anything unusual. If the storm clouds weren't so obviously brewing, it would have been fun.

By noon, the sky was as dark as midnight. We decided we should quickly stop for lunch so that Jo and Hanna could have a break from working the boat's controls.

We tied up to the nearest island and hopped out to stretch our legs.

Hanna brought out more of the spice cake and water, but this time she added candied chestnuts and dried fruits as well.

Just as we were finishing up, a bunch of lightning bugs circled our camp.

"That's strange," said Jo.

"Yeah," said Hanna. "What could these guys want?"

The lightning bugs turned and made a flashing straight line into the trees.

"Looks like they want us to go in there," I said.

"I dunno. We should be getting back to the boat. Those clouds look bad," said Jo.

"I vote we investigate. What if they're trying to help us somehow?" said Hanna.

I stood up and brushed off my pants. "Let's check it out," I said.

Jo began to protest.

"Quickly," I added.

We followed the line of little blinking lights into the trees. A misting rain began to fall and I noticed more clumps of orange goop here than I had at our camp that morning. The lights ended up in the high branches of a cypress.

At first everything looked the same—clumps of twigs and leaves.

Hanna rubbed her eyes. She was the first to see what Jo and I couldn't. "Is that a face up there? In the leaves?"

The lightning bugs encircled us in a glowing wreath of excitement.

Hanna turned to me and said, "You're in charge. I think the bugs want you to do something about whatever's up there."

"They don't like to be called just bugs, Hanna, you know that," Jo said. Then she turned to me. "She's right, though. You're in charge. What do you think we should do?"

Once again my fingers closed around the necklace. What should I do?

Clinging to the shell hanging around my neck, I whispered to Hanna and Jo, "Can you fly up and tell me what that is?"

The twin fairies lifted off. I felt my entire body stiffen as they drew nearer to the unmoving face pressed firmly between the leaves and the twigs.

Just as they were close enough to touch the face, the eyes opened.

The mouth opened and let out a scream.

Hanna and Jo tumbled backward, and I started screaming, too.

PLUNK! PLUNK! PLUNK!

Down a body fell. Out of the tree and onto a bed of leaves. A camouflage blanket of moss and leaves fell away to reveal a small boy. He looked like he might have been all of five years old.

"'Elp! 'Elp! Them fairies is trying to kill me!" he cried. His voice was high and girly, but he had big hands and big feet and long, thin legs.

Hanna and Jo landed beside me.

This terrified the boy. He started screaming even louder and picked up a stick like he was going to attack us.

Not to be outdone, Hanna picked up a bigger stick and swung it threateningly.

I could tell she wasn't really aiming for him, but

unfortunately he chose that moment to leap forward and took a big hit to his side. It knocked him clear over.

"Yow!" he yelled.

"Sorry!" cried Hanna.

"Why are you hitting him?" yelled Jo.

We all stood panting and staring bug-eyed at each other, with the rain streaking our faces.

"Okay," I said. "Can we just take a breath and figure out what's going on? Who are you? Why are you here?" I took a step toward him.

"Wait!" said Jo. "Lilu, Dragonfly Fairies specialize in creating magical shields. Our magic will protect us from ordinary creatures of the marsh like bobcats or snakes, but other magical creatures . . ." She shifted her gaze to Moss Boy. "It's like the marsh frogs. Bad magic can hurt you. And if you invite it in, we cannot protect you."

I looked at the cowering boy. Now the mask of moss and leaves had fallen away in a clump. Stooping slowly, I picked up his mask. I could have sworn something about him had changed since he'd fallen. Something more than losing his leaves.

"I mean ya no 'arm, really,"

he said. "I'm lost and alone. I don't wanna be alone."

I turned to Hanna and Jo. An assortment of lightning bugs flew in tiny formations, zooming north, then south, east, then west.

"Turning our back on someone who is lost and afraid can't be the right thing to do in Aventurine—or anyplace else," I said. I dropped the mask. What would Tandy do?

Overhead, thunder shook the clouds, and the thin mist fell even harder and faster.

"Come on, let's get back to the boat," I said.

No one moved.

"Move!" I said with a grunt, grabbing hold of the strange boy's hand and dragging him along before I could think about it.

His name was Anansi. It sounded oddly familiar to me, this name, but then I figured that was silly. Clearly I'd never met Moss Boy—Anansi—before.

Back at the boat we quickly started a fire, since Anansi seemed to be freezing and couldn't stop shaking. At first he concentrated on eating everything in sight. He gobbled and slurped and chewed and chomped. Then he began to tell his story. He said he'd gotten separated from his family. They lived in the marsh, and he'd fallen asleep in the tree. His family had sensed the

Tangerine Tide brewing and had left for their storm shelter in the night, accidentally leaving him behind. They must have been sick with worry by now.

Thinking about missing family, I touched my shell necklace again.

"What's that you've got?" Anansi asked, reaching for it.

I instinctively pulled away, but then felt guilty. I moved closer and held the necklace up for him to see. "A shell. It reminds me of my sister."

"A twin," he said with a nod.

"How did you know I was a twin?" I frowned.

Anansi paused and tilted his head to one side. Then he scuttled away from me. When he moved, he walked with a hitch. Like he might at any moment start moving sideways. It was odd, yet something about it was almost funny.

"I know 'cause I see it in your eyes," he said. "Did ya know that twins are a powerful, magical thing?"

I nodded, remembering my conversation with Mom about Mama Akuko.

Anansi gestured toward my shell. "Your sister, she's in there, waiting if ya should need her power. But ya won't. Ya could take that off right now and be fine!"

I smiled, and he scurried closer to me. Then he

reached for the necklace. Reached for the shell. To take Tandy away from me.

"We really should be going now!" Jo moved around the campfire and stepped between Anansi and me.

His eyes grew large and round. Anansi dropped his head like he was caught doing something bad. "I didn't mean to offend ya," he said. He made a pouty face that was just about the silliest-looking thing you could imagine.

I laughed and patted him on the shoulder. "No harm done," I said.

The tension eased out of the group.

As Hanna and Jo made sure the fire was out and that all of our belongings were stored away, I told Anansi about our journey. "We're going to the Castle on Stilts. Jo and Hanna are my guides," I said.

"And we're trying to beat the Tangerine Tide, so speed is of the essence," Jo added, with a meaningful look.

Everything was loaded up and ready to go. The sky was getting even blacker. Any minute now, the magical hurricane might be upon us; I could feel it.

I turned to Anansi and said, "I hope you find your

family. Is there anything more we can do to help?"

"'Ow are ya gettin' to the Castle on Stilts?" he asked.

Jo, who was uncoiling the rope from the fat belly of a tree trunk, turned and pointed east across the water.

Anansi frowned. "But that'll take ya too long. If ya wanna get there before the storm hits, I know a better way."

Jo, Hanna, and I exchanged uncertain looks.

Finally, Hanna shrugged. "A shortcut would be awesome," she said.

"I don't know, Hanna. Our current path will get us there." Jo's wings fluttered with concern.

Hanna tapped a finger to her lips, considering. "Yes, but we don't know if the storm will break before our path gets us there. We should take the risk."

They went back and forth like that for a minute; then once again they turned to me. Jo said, "It's Lilu's decision."

"And Lilu wants us to get there as soon as possible," Hanna said. "Right, Lilu?"

"You're sure you know a shortcut?" I asked Anansi.

He nodded enthusiastically. "It's on my way. I

can ride on the boat with ya and show ya the way. It won't take long 't all."

So we climbed aboard — Anansi standing with Jo, pointing out the way. As I sat beside Hanna, I was glad that I had made a decision. At least we were moving again.

I looked back at Anansi and couldn't help wondering again, *Why does his name sound so familiar?*

8

The Trickster

The rain returned, and though the ba-dum boat's canopy protected our bodies, it couldn't keep our spirits from dampening. As we followed Anansi's directions, we began to pass larger sections of the marsh with the orange goop floating on the surface like a nasty oil spill.

After a few hours of travel, Anansi shouted, "We're here!"

But where was here?

We seemed to still be deep in the belly of the marsh. Hanna and Jo looked tired as they lowered the boat onto a mushy lip of land. They didn't want to waste energy flying, so I helped the twin fairies down and tied up the lines. Then we stood, gawking up at the most incredibly wide, gnarled, twisted tree I'd ever seen.

A sick, hollow feeling settled into my gut.

The tree stood off a short distance from the marsh. It was so wide that if we all held hands and pressed ourselves against the trunk, we'd only reach a third of the way around. Surrounding the giant tree was a mysterious greenish glow. The eerie light flickered constantly and cast terrifying shadows around us.

"What is this place?" Hanna said.

I turned to Anansi, expecting him to explain, but what I saw left me speechless.

He was grinning.

And he wasn't a boy anymore.

Remember how I said he'd been holding himself in a funny way that made him walk sort of weird? Well, you'd walk weird, too, if you were trying to hide eight legs inside your clothes!

"He's a spider!" I gasped.

Hanna and Jo screamed and tried to fly back into the boat. It hit me that spiders eat dragonflies.

Had I invited the enemy onto our trip?

Anansi didn't attack, though. He turned and danced up the gigantic tree. All eight of his legs moved gracefully now that they were free of his clothing. He quickly climbed higher and higher.

Seeing him in his true form, I rolled his name around in my head. *Anansi . . . Anansi . . . Anansi!*

"I know where I've heard his name before," I said.

Hanna and Jo glanced at me but quickly turned back to watch the spider as he climbed.

"Look." Hanna pointed.

Then I saw it, too. A rickety old house sat in the crook of the tree's limbs.

It looked menacing, definitely not a castle on stilts.

I gulped.

Nan-Nan had told Tan and me plenty of stories about the spider Anansi. He's a popular character in African folklore. His tricks are legendary. I couldn't believe I'd been dumb enough to fall for one!

"What is it?" Jo asked.

I shook my head.

Atop the tree limbs, the tiny old shack began to quake. Anansi paused in his climb. A thunderous boom sent us to our knees, but it didn't come from the sky; it came from the shack.

"Lilu, what is it? What do you know?" Jo had moved closer. She was right at my side. I lowered my head. How could I tell her? I felt so ashamed. Nan-Nan had taken so much pride in her stories. All of my female relatives had. Now it was like I was on her porch, hearing the story of Anansi in my head all over again.

"Please tell us," said Jo quietly.

"Anansi is not only a spider; he's also a trickster," I said. "He loved storytelling so much, he wanted to have all the stories in the world. So his father, the Sky God, gave him a near-impossible task. He said, 'Bring back Onini the python, Osebo the leopard, the Mmoboro hornets, and Mmoatia the invisible fairy, and I will give you what your heart desires.' Anansi was clever. But this task might have been his match."

Now Jo and Hanna stood together facing me. Backlit by the eerie green glow, their ebony skin looked ashen.

In the tree, thunder continued to boom from the house, and Anansi appeared uncertain. His long, thin legs clung to the bark.

"So what did Anansi do?" Jo urged.

"Too bad he didn't get eaten by the python. If he had, we might be at Queen Alaina's now, rather than here trying to figure out how to squash an evil spider hiding up in a big, fat tree!" Hanna said.

I laughed, but there wasn't much funny about our situation.

As if reading my thoughts, Jo said, "We have to get that trickster out of the tree. We have to make him come down here and tell us how to get to the castle."

Hanna turned to me and placed her hand on my

arm. "Please, Lilu, tell us what happened in your story."

So I finished. I told them what Nan-Nan had told me. That Anansi devised several clever ruses to capture the creatures one by one until he had them all. Then he delivered them to his father, who honored his promise and turned over all the stories.

Hanna said, "So how does this help us? What does the story mean?"

She'd voiced exactly how I'd felt each time Nan-Nan had told the story. Believe me, Nan-Nan had told it more than once, which was why I felt like such a loser for not remembering Anansi's name sooner.

"Every time I'd complain that I didn't learn something as fast as Tandy, Nan-Nan would tell the story of Anansi. And at the end, she'd always say the same thing: 'Child, you have the power to do the impossible, just like that ol' spider. All that matters is that you believe in yourself and that you're willing to fight for what you want.' "

It'd been a long time since she'd told me that story. Come to think of it, not since I'd started diving. I guess that was the first time I'd set out to make myself really good at anything.

A guilty tickle scratched at my heart. Learning to be a good diver had been easy—at first, anyway—

because Tan was there, leading the way.

I closed my hand around my crescent moon shell. I should never have made such an important decision—following Anansi's shortcut—on my own. I was in way over my head.

Condiga! Condiga! Condiga! I called.

What kind of danger are you in? Tandy answered. Her voice was so close, it was as if she'd come through the shell and was sprinkled in the air around me.

I made the decision to follow a stranger, Anansi, who turned out to be the trickster. Now we're lost in the marsh, and if we don't find our way out soon and reach our destination, very bad things will happen. What should I do?

The misting rain began to fall harder. Fat drops plunged through the air and drenched us.

You weren't wrong. Anansi knows the way. Ask the thunder. Take care of the thunder, and thunder will take care of you.

I could feel the connection cutting off. *Wait!* I called. But it was gone.

Oh, boy! Was it because my sister was talking to me through a seashell that she'd started sounding like some sort of spirit guide? How was I supposed to ask the thunder?

"Tandy says I have to talk to the thunder."

"That's weird," said Jo, eyeing my necklace and then turning back to the tree. "You mean whoever's shaking that old house?"

"Then hurry!" said Hanna. "We'll protect the boat by pulling it back into the trees over there. Remember, if we don't leave soon we'll never make it to the Castle on Stilts in time to save the crane egg. Zandria and Zeus will lose their baby."

I stared up at the tree, and then threw back my shoulders. If I could do a forward flying two-and-a-half somersault dive in competition, then I could do this.

I strode up to the tree and found a craggy foothold to step into, then began to climb. The bark was slick. I only made it a few steps before I slid down again.

Looking up, I could barely make out Anansi staring down at me. His expression was a mixture of puzzlement and terror. Was he truly afraid? Or was it simply another trick?

"Keep trying!" yelled the fairies. Their voices were almost buried beneath the heavy patter of the rain and thunder.

Pressing my body against the side of the tree, carefully, very carefully, I began to inch my way up.

Hand. Foot. Hand. Foot. *Scoot.* Hand. Foot. Hand. Foot. *Scoot.*

The tree shook every time the thunder boomed.

My fingers ached from searching out handholds and gripping the bark. My neck was stiff, and my thighs burned from trying to push myself higher and higher with each climb. I took a deep breath. Tandy had never steered me wrong. I had to do this. I just wished I had a rope.

I reached a deep knothole and found a relatively stable perch. Carefully, I stretched out my fingers into the falling rain. It reflected greenish in the dim light. The feel of it was cool and strangely solid, like actual beads.

I concentrated on the drops and twirled them around in my fingers. The droplets began to solidify and knit together, forming a perfect, iridescent string of beads. This I could work with!

In my excitement, I leaned out a little too far and felt myself swaying. I was losing my footing in the knothole!

Heart pounding, rain pouring from the inky sky, I replanted my foot firmly in the tree's crevice and steadied myself. Then I reached out again and began catching and twirling more and more droplets, yanking them in as I went. I had to keep my focus trained on the beads at all times, but soon enough, I had a long rope made of lumpy raindrops.

I had to work fast. Knotting a loop in the watery rope, I tossed it across a branch outside the doorstep of the rickety house, catching it on a clump of leaves.

Now was the moment of faith. If I let go of the tree's trunk to take hold of the rope with both hands, I'd have to rely solely on it. I'd have to truly believe it would hold.

I took a deep breath and put all of my body weight on the rope. It held! Carefully, I began to pull myself up.

Inch by inch I climbed. Eventually, I was so high up, the calls of encouragement from the fairies faded.

Anansi eyed me from across the tree. I was higher than him now, but we were too far from each other to touch. Thunder crackled around us. Anansi shut his eyes and trembled.

I swallowed hard and continued. When I finally reached the end of my rope, I wanted to shout with excitement, but there was no time. I stood on the slick branch and knocked at the house's door.

How could anyone hear my knocks over the cacophony of sound in there?

Then a strong gust of wind sucked open the door, and I was propelled inside. The door slammed shut behind me.

A tiny woman with a dangerous scowl spun

around to face me. She opened her mouth and—
BOOM!—thunder roared like a mountain lion.

"Hurry!" she boomed. Her skin was white, and
her long gray dress swirled and piled around her like
an angry storm cloud. Right before she let out another
resounding boom, lightning snaked down the chim-
ney and into the fireplace.

"Owww!" cried Thunder. Her black eyes were
flecked with electricity. She stared intently at me,
then winced as though something heavy had fallen on
her foot.

I had been so terrified by the woman's thundering
that I hadn't noticed—she wasn't angry at all. She was
in pain.

"My tooth! My tooth! My blasted tooth!" she
boomed.

"Are . . . are you thunder?"

"I am Oya, goddess of thunder, wind, and
lightning."

The entire house swayed just a bit, and I took
the hint and dropped into a curtsy.

Oya's furrowed brows relaxed a bit. She seemed
like she'd been waiting for me.

Now that my eyes had adjusted to the light, I
saw the goddess more clearly. In addition to wearing
a dress of storm clouds, she wore a necklace of rain

beads and hailstones that glittered like gems. And her hair—her hair was truly awesome.

My mother had told me about Medusa, an evil figure in Greek mythology who had snakes for hair and could turn a person to stone just by looking at them. Oya hadn't turned me to stone, but her hair was made of lightning bolts that zapped and sizzled around her face and down her back.

"Stop staring at my blasted head. I'm in agony! I've tried and tried, and I can't do anything about this tooth. Now, you promised my nephew you'd help, otherwise you wouldn't be here, so help!"

Whoa! Oya was way, way confused.

"I'm sorry you're in pain, but who's your nephew?"

The hearth came alive with lightning fire, hot and bright. The boom that followed caused me to jump backward and stumble against a loose floorboard. I fell to the side and landed ungracefully on my hip with the wooden totem in my pocket. I quickly stood, rubbing my hip and unable to rub what was really hurting— my pride.

"Um, like I was saying, I don't know your nephew. I'm trying . . ." I took a deep breath. Started again. "We need to get to the Castle on Stilts. Before the Tangerine Tide. That trickster, Anansi, told us he was taking us on a shortcut to the castle. Instead, we wound up here."

When she scowled, her hair rose up on its ends and her dark eyes crackled. She shouted, "Anansiiiiiiii!"

BOOM! BOOM! BOOM!

Anansi scuttled in the doorway behind me.

"Explain quickly, Anansi. I'm hurting. And none of your stories, now. Just the straight truth, or I'll singe you," said Oya. She turned to me. "He has stories crowding his brain. He can't help but try them out on everyone he meets."

Anansi explained, with darting glances at Oya, that she had sent him to find me when she'd heard I was nearby. "When a big ol' goddess gets a toothache, she can't just go to a regular doctor, now can she? She's gotta get some magical doctorin'. And we all know in Aventurine that fairy-godmothers-in-training are the ones with the most powerful magic. So I got ya to come!" he said.

The idea that I had more powerful magic than others made me feel dizzy. As much as I'd grown accustomed to Tan leading the way, part of me secretly longed to be as strong and in charge as she was. Now I felt ripples of

fear tickling my spine. Having power was a lot of responsibility. Sometimes a frightening responsibility.

"My auntie's teeth are very strong. She 'as quite
a bite." Anansi's voice cut into my thoughts. He was
edging away from Oya as if he was frightened of her.
"Only someone wit' your power can use the elements
to 'elp 'er."

I wasn't quite over being angry at him. "Tricking
me to get your way was not cool, Anansi. You should
have come right out and asked for help."

Anansi hung his head and seemed to grow smaller,
but it was impossible to tell if he was really contrite.

I turned back to Oya. She looked pretty miserable.
I guess I couldn't stay mad at Anansi, knowing that if
Tandy were sick, I might try to trick people into helping
her, too.

I approached the thunder goddess, staying away
from her hair. "Can I look at the tooth?" I asked.

She eagerly opened her mouth wide so that
I could see the rotting molar and its inflamed gums.
The tooth looked angry and painful.

"I have an idea, but it might hurt you a bit before
it feels better. Can I have a few strands of your hair?"

Oya looked worried, but she reached up and
pulled out three long lightning bolts, then handed
them to me.

The lightning jumped and curled in my hand. I could sense that it wanted to leap out and strike something. It felt icy hot in my grip.

My fingers worked quickly. I focused on the electricity, imagining it knitting into solid metal. I was much faster this time than I'd been with the masks I'd made for Jo and Hanna. Soon links of a lightning chain grew under my touch. When the bolts were gone, I held up a chain as thin as a strand of hair but as strong as iron. It sizzled and gleamed in my hand.

Anansi had changed back to a boy while I was focused on my work. "Ya almost done now," he said, his eyes shining.

I paused. "If I help you, do you promise to be honest with me? No more lies. We have to make it to the Castle on Stilts before the storm. Is there a quick way to get back on the right path from here?"

Anansi smiled. "The shortcut is real; I just didn't take you all the way. I will show you."

He motioned for me to continue, but I shook my head. The lightning was beginning to grow hotter in my hand. "How can I trust you?" I asked.

"You can't trust him, but you can trust me," said Oya. "Do this for me, and I will speak with his father, the Sky God. We will make sure that you get to your destination."

"Wait. Can you or the Sky God stop the Tangerine Tide?"

BOOM!

Oya doubled over with pain. She shook her head. "We must not. That is forbidden. All magic must run its course," she said.

I finished the chain, creating a loop at the end, and then offered that end to Anansi. "Loop this around your aunt's tooth," I said.

Anansi took the end and then dropped it. "Yow!" he cried. "That's hot!"

He grabbed it again. This time he didn't drop it. When he placed the loop over her tooth, I heard a slight sizzle. Oya moaned.

Before any of us could think too much about it, I yanked.

Air crackled in the small house. My arm felt a hundred times stronger than it ever had. The thin links of the chain strained, then—*SWAK!*—out flew her molar.

I toppled—again—and landed in another embarrassing heap on the knotty-pine floor. It seemed I had the power to weave perfume, bead rain, and twist lightning, but I was still having trouble with basic gravity.

This time Anansi and Oya helped me to my feet,

but not before I pulled the totem that Queen Patchouli had given me out of my pocket to make sure it had survived my latest fall. Now the carvings on the totem glowed and sparkled. The air filled with what looked like the fairy dust in the movie *Peter Pan*. I'd have to remember to ask Hanna and Jo how a magical totem worked.

"It's the totem of trust," Anansi said in a hushed voice.

Oya rubbed her cheek. When she opened her mouth, there was no *BOOM!*—just a soft rumble. She smiled.

Suddenly, out of the lion's mouth on the totem shone a light, like a movie projector. Two figures stood before us. One figure was a strong-looking male who shone with an inner fire, hot and blinding. He wore a lion's mane around his neck and other furs and skins that I could not name on the rest of his body— it was too hard to look at him or his clothing for long. The other figure was easier to look at. She glowed with a cool light and was dressed in white crocodile skin. She looked mysterious and did not smile as openly as the man.

"The Sun God and the Moon Goddess. They are here to guide you," Oya said. "Queen Patchouli gave you this totem, yes?"

I nodded.

"By helping me, despite the tricks of Anansi, you have unlocked the totem's power. It is your destiny to use this totem wisely, Lilu. Take care, for you may only call upon each god once. Be wise with your choices."

"I will, I promise," I whispered. I was shocked that Queen Patchouli had given me such a powerful gift.

The figures of the gods faded, and I tucked the totem back into my pocket. I couldn't believe how many times I'd fallen on and bumped this precious gift. I would take better care of it from now on.

"Good. Now get along. I will alert the Sky God and keep the hurricane back for a bit, since you lost time on my account," said Oya.

"Come! I'll show ya the way." Anansi was back in spider form. He stepped closer and offered me his back. I didn't want to touch him as a spider, but I didn't want him to notice my hesitation, either. I climbed onto his bristly back with a slight shudder and waved good-bye to Oya. Then we headed down the tree.

Hanna and Jo cheered when they saw me climb

from Anansi's back at the base of the tree. It felt good that they were so clearly glad to see me. Unfortunately, they were also terrified of Anansi in his spider form. Something to do with being Dragonfly Fairies, I'm sure.

They kept the boat between themselves and Anansi. I quickly recapped what had happened up in the house with Oya and Anansi. Both Hanna and Jo were impressed that my totem could contact the Sun God and the Moon Goddess.

"So, Anansi," I said, turning to him, "how do we *really* get to the Castle on Stilts?"

With the flick of one of his legs, a line of mist illuminated and stretched past the trees and out into the marsh. "The mist will lead ya out into the salt marsh. If ya move swiftly, ya should reach the beach side of the marsh by sunrise. Follow the mist, and it'll lead ya all the way."

Once again, Hanna, Jo, and I were back in the ba-dum boat. This time, the destination had never been so tantalizingly close.

9

Inside the Castle

My senses awoke one by one, and I realized I had fallen asleep. I rolled over slowly and saw Jo steering the boat. Hanna was curled up asleep. The drums were on autopilot.

Jo smiled at me. "We're almost there," she said.

Oya and the Sky God had worked some magic. Blue sky and flat waters stretched out to meet each other. Hundreds of tufted white clouds, like perfectly fluffed pillows, hung suspended above us. The air was so calm it was hard to imagine that the Tangerine Tide was on its way. It looked like the kind of day you'd want to spend at the beach, swimming in the ocean, hanging out with your family and friends. It looked so . . . *perfect.*

If I'd learned anything from Anansi, it was that looks could be deceiving.

"Want me to take over?" I asked, sitting up with a yawn.

Jo shrugged. "I'm fine."

We skimmed along on the brackish water. I ran my fingers over the front of the crescent moon shell hanging from my neck. Being in Aventurine, on this journey—it was like time had both slowed down and sped up. Everything was happening really fast, but being able to follow in Mom's footsteps and becoming a fairy godmother was like watching a film in my mind playing in slow motion. The only missing piece to make things perfect was Tandy. If she and I became fairy godmothers at the same time, I knew it would bring us back together.

"You miss her, right?" Jo's tone was matter-of-fact as she steered the boat toward open water. She looked at my fingers resting on the shell.

I nodded. "Yeah, I just wish she were here."

"Why?"

We both glanced at Hanna, who was snuggled into a ball. I blew out a sigh. And just like that, I was able to say to Jo things I hadn't been able to say out loud to anyone. I told her how close Tan and I used to be, how close our *family* used to be. We had done everything together. I told her how devastated I'd been when my parents divorced. How I was the only one who had cried. Tan had said she wasn't surprised about the divorce. How could she have said such a thing?

"Mom isn't happy, Lilu, you know that!" she'd said.

I hadn't seen it that way. That was when I'd become convinced that it was up to Tan and me to get them back together. Only Tan didn't seem interested in doing that.

"Don't you think maybe your sister deserves to try something new?" Jo asked. I had just been telling her how much I'd hoped the dive meet would be the thing that would bring us all closer together. But Tan had been so caught up in getting her part in the play, she'd barely noticed.

"You don't get it, Jo. You and Hanna act so opposite sometimes. You're more cautious and thoughtful, and Hanna is so adventurous, you know? But it was never like that with Tan and me. We were so close, it was like we were the same person."

Jo took a step toward me, her bright blue eyes flashing. "But you're two people, not one," she said. "Wouldn't you rather be both sides of one whole person than be one person broken in half? You have no idea. . . . Sounds like your sister is trying to build herself up. What about you?"

Her beautiful ebony face was a mask of raw emotion. Was that really how Tan felt? Did she think I was trying to keep her from being a whole person?

"We're here!" Hanna said, awake and breaking the awful spell of Jo's intensity. How long had she been listening?

The feelings that rushed up under my skin were like itchy hives. Jo was wrong! Tan and I *were* like one person; we'd been happy like that. And we could be that way again.

Couldn't we?

Hanna took to the drums, and the boat sped up. I slid away from the gut-clenching gaze of Jo and looked out at the sandy shore of the salt marsh. A silhouette of a shanty stood in the distance. It looked so fragile.

"I pictured a huge castle, magically supported by stilts," I said, desperate to talk about something else.

Hanna laughed. "Just wait. Outsides don't always match insides."

The boat was over shallow water now. Hanna and Jo skillfully maneuvered it up to the beach and brought it down to rest. When we got out, we cheered and high-fived each other. We'd finally made it! The Castle on Stilts loomed just a few feet ahead, with a rickety stairway leading from the sand to the doorway.

We rushed up the stairs, so happy to have arrived.

The door flew open, and a blue-tinged woman wearing a kimono-style silk robe held out her arms and said, "Jo and Hanna! Lilu! Welcome to my Castle on Stilts. I am Queen Alaina. Follow me, please. We're all very happy you've finally arrived."

From the outside, the Castle on Stilts looked like an abandoned beach house. The staircase was weathered and groaned with each step. I'd seen spiderwebs that looked sturdier than the castle.

Inside, though, it was totally different. The ceiling arched two stories high with a shining chandelier of magically frozen icicles. Glittering sapphire floors stretched down a hallway into the distance. This truly *was* a castle. No question.

"How can this be?" I asked in awe.

"Um, duh, magic!" said Hanna with an exaggerated eye roll.

Jo and I laughed.

We moved swiftly across the gleaming floor, past benches of carved gems, which I really wanted to stop and admire, to the end of the hallway and two big wooden doors. Queen Alaina thrust open the doors and continued into an enormous room with stunning stained-glass windows.

But the windows were not the most amazing thing.

The room was bursting with animals!

The birds were most noticeable at first; herons, storks, and black ducks were perched on benches and clustered in corners. They all were familiar-looking but had a hint of magic about them. When the black ducks noticed my entrance, they went into a shadowy corner and completely disappeared. I couldn't help laughing; they had more to fear from the alligators than from me!

Yes, that's right, there were alligators—BIG alligators—stretched out in patches of colored light from the stained-glass windows. There were also snakes, turtles, and frogs (although no marsh frogs, thankfully), raccoons, rabbits, skunks, opossums, bobcats, deer, and panthers.

Jo stopped. She clearly wanted to turn and run away. I could tell Hanna wasn't very excited about walking into a room of alligators, either. Her face had gone a shade paler; her green eyes were wide with fear. "Um, Queen Alaina, what's going on here?" she called above the cacophony.

"Follow me, and I'll show you," said Queen Alaina. She tapped a panther's back as we walked by. It was crouched down and slowly stalking toward a group of herons. "You know the rule," she said.

The big cat immediately began licking its tail, as if it had not been about to pounce on unsuspecting fowl.

I wondered what rule she meant. But leave it to a cat to look offended when it was caught breaking it!

The fairy queen led us to a much smaller door. She opened it and motioned us through, then shut it behind us.

We were at the back end of the castle, near a wall of windows overlooking the sea. Waves hiccupped from the ocean side of the marshland. It was starting now, I thought, and my heart jittered with a jolt of adrenaline. When I'd been on the diving board trying to remember to breathe and concentrate on my approach, the idea of messing up had made my heart buzz in my chest. That was nothing compared to what I felt as I stared at the growing waves and dark clouds building up along the shore of Aventurine.

I turned away from the windows and studied the others in the room. Fairies resembling Hanna and Jo were sitting at a long table, weaving something. Most were dressed a lot more simply than my fairy friends. The majority of the fairies favored kimono-style robes similar to their queen's outfit, though not as richly detailed.

I had been secretly eyeing the queen's kimono. The fabric had living plants and animals moving about it! Birds flew, alligators swam, and all of it was occurring right in the fabric that the queen wore. If only *I* could weave like that!

The queen noticed me staring. "It was a gift from Queen Patchouli. The finest Willowood cloth yet. She and I are good friends, and we have a bit of a friendly competition when it comes to weaving," she said.

I smiled. I understood competition over weaving, of course—I was usually the sister who came up short. "What did you mean by 'rule' back there?" I asked.

"With the threat of the Tangerine Tide hanging over the marsh, I've invited the animals into my castle for protection. The rule is that they are not allowed to hunt other animals who have also come to my castle for protection. We will provide them with any food they need. Some have taken me up on my offer. I wish more would come. These Dragonfly Fairies are helping me to prepare that protection now," she said, and nodded for me to sit at the table with the fairies.

I saw immediately that they were weaving a net. Dragonflies were flying in and out of an open window and returning with beads, which were being woven into the net. But why?

"Are you trying to capture the hurricane?" I asked.

The Dragonfly Fairies nearby chuckled.

"No, magic must run its course, but we're weaving this net to shield our castle. These beads of sea-water are being spelled with strong protections to keep the destructive magic of the hurricane from breaking through." Queen Alaina sighed. "Even though I've made the castle as small as it will go, there's still quite a lot of work to do before the shield is ready. And I fear the hurricane will reach us before we have the net in place."

A hushed whisper filled the room. I could tell that the fairies didn't like hearing such negative news from their queen.

"Well, we're here now," said Hanna. "And we've brought Lilu. She's way more talented than any other weaver I know. She'll help us meet the deadline. I know she—"

"But what about our mission, Hanna?" interrupted Jo. "We need to get Lilu and the egg back to Zeus and Zandria first, right?"

Hanna bit her lip and didn't say anything.

Queen Alaina waved a fairy over. The fairy pushed a huge basket of woven golden branches before her. When it got closer, I could see that it wasn't really a basket. It was more like . . . *a nest!*

I peered into the golden nest and was immediately alarmed. The whooping crane egg did not look whole and perfect like I had imagined—a tiny crack was beginning to form.

"He is ready to come into the world," said the fairy who had pushed the nest forward. She had long eyelashes studded with shimmering crystals. "I've helped all I could to keep this little one safe. Now time is working against us."

"If you don't get him back to his family by tomorrow, it'll be too late. He'll hatch without his parents and will never recognize them," Queen Alaina said.

Jo and Hanna, for the first time since I'd met them, fluttered their wings nervously as they stood nearby.

"Come, Lilu. You need a shower and breakfast. We have much to do and not much time."

The shower turned out to be a waterfall—a

waterfall!—inside the castle. A glistening blue wall of Aventurine stone provided the backdrop as the water rushed down. I expected it to be ice-cold, but it changed quickly from icy to warm.

I came out of the shower feeling like a year of dirt and all of my weariness had disappeared down the drain. My clothes had been cleaned while I was away. On top were my totem and the water lilies—I had refused to take off my crescent moon shell.

I quickly dressed and stuck the totem back into my pocket and the water lilies behind my right ear.

I didn't know how hungry I was until I reached the dining area. A long wooden plank with stone-carved legs held the most scrumptious array of fruits and veggies—cantaloupe, honeydew melon, pink watermelon smiles, baskets filled with bright red strawberries, cucumbers and carrots sliced and placed in smaller baskets. It was embarrassing how fast I gobbled it up, but I couldn't help myself.

"You sure don't eat like a bird," said Hanna.

She and Jo sat down on the bench beside me and smiled. They looked shiny and scrubbed clean, too. I was relieved to see their familiar faces in the sea of Dragonfly Fairies flitting about.

"What're we going to do, Lilu?" asked Jo.

"Yeah," said Hanna, "are we heading back? Or do you want to help weave the shield?"

This was not an easy decision. My mission was to get the egg and bring it back to the Willowood. I wasn't supposed to stay and help with things here. But it felt wrong to abandon them, especially after seeing all of the animals and the Dragonfly Fairies.

"I think we should stay as long as we can to help. Then we'll leave and bring the egg to its parents really fast — no detours."

Hanna laughed. "I wish we could've just avoided detours the first time around," she said.

"Me too. Anansi turned out okay, I guess, but I hate spiders," said Jo with a shiver.

I tapped the totem in my pocket. "I dunno. That detour might've turned out to be useful," I said.

"If you say so. Let's go tell Queen Alaina that we're going to help with the shield," said Hanna.

We found our way back to the room with the windows to the sea. The clouds were darker and flashing orange now. I quickly found a spot at the table. The sooner this shield was finished, the sooner we could take the egg and complete our mission.

Everyone was hard at work; the only sounds were the steady buzz of dragonflies and the shuffle and clack of fairies weaving the net at an urgent pace. The fairy next to me, Willia, showed me the simple weave pattern. She spelled the sea beads before I added them to the net.

At first I was all thumbs. I kept glancing up to see if the fairies were watching me and thinking I was an embarrassment to the Songa Lineage. But they were all working too hard to care about my not being the most skillful weaver. Once I realized no one was judging me, I settled into an easy routine with Willia.

Over, under. Over, under. Slip on a bead. Over, under. Over, under. Slip on a bead.

We worked like that for hours. Time sped by. Someone placed a crusty slice of bread next to me at one point. It was spread with delicious jam that fizzed in my mouth and filled my stomach. Another time a hot tea drink appeared. It had leaves floating in it. I accidentally ate one and it tasted like Red Hots. The warm cup in my hands loosened my cramping fingers, and with the spiced leaves shocking my tongue, I felt much more awake.

At the beginning, my fingers had felt too large and stiff. I struggled to get the threads to move the way I wanted them to. But unlike at Nan-Nan's, where by now I'd have stalked off, overwhelmed with trying to keep up with everyone else, I kept working. It was different here. I wasn't part of a set, a twin trying to hold her own against a look-alike. Here I was just . . . me. A girl who wasn't quite a pro at weaving, but who got better and better as the day wore on.

Every once in a while, I would look up and see how much brighter the orange flickers in the clouds had grown. The wind had picked up and the storm no longer looked like it would hit tomorrow; it looked like it would hit tonight.

I thought the most immediate problem was the storm. I was wrong.

We all heard the crack at the same time.

Jo, Hanna, Queen Alaina, and I rushed over to the golden nest. There was no doubt that the sound had come from the egg.

The crack was growing, and it looked like the baby might hatch sooner than expected.

"If only we could find a way to hold it together, even for a short while," Hanna said.

"We need to hold it together and keep it warm. If it's warm enough inside the shell and the shell is firmly around it, the baby might calm down and cease squirming," Jo replied.

Maybe . . . I sprinted toward the door.

"Where are you going?" called Queen Alaina.

"I have an idea! I'll be right back!" I shouted, aware that I was being a bit rude to a queen, but knowing I had to move fast.

The rickety steps rattled under my feet as I raced out of the Castle on Stilts. The air outside felt thick, heavy. I ran toward a sunny patch on the side of the beach facing the marsh and away from the ocean. Here there were a few clouds, but nothing like what was brewing out at sea.

I fished in my pocket and pulled out the totem. Twirling it toward the sky, I watched as the fairy dust began to rain down on me once again. Sparkling dots of light sprinkled the air. The lion's mouth shone its light again, and I watched as first the outlines, then the shapes of the two gods appeared and solidified. The Sun God and the Moon Goddess.

What should I say?

I decided to just blurt it out. "I need your help. I'd like to use the sun's beams and weave them into a warm blanket that is tight enough to hold together the shell of an egg. Please help me."

The Sun God's smile broadened. He began to glow more and more brightly, until I felt like I would be able to see only bright lights forever. I held up a hand to shield my eyes, and the rays divided into shafts of light. I gripped the rays and pulled them close to my chest. Unlike the sizzling lightning, the sun's light felt like soft blades of warm, strong grass.

I sank to my knees in the sand. Unlike inside the castle, however, where my fingers sometimes felt numb or uncertain, out here, holding the sun's rays, I didn't even think about it — I just worked. I focused on the rays of light and thought about how I would weave a blanket of long grasses. My fingers moved faster and faster. A sparkling blanket began to form. Luckily it didn't have to be big enough to cover a castle — just an egg.

Eventually I was holding a shining blanket.

I bowed to the Sun God. "Thank you for letting me use your rays," I said.

The Sun God and the Moon Goddess both faded away.

I folded the blanket and stuffed the totem back into my pocket. Then I leapt up and climbed the stairs, ran through the long hallway and the crowded room of animals, and made my way into the room by the sea. Hanna, Jo, and Queen Alaina stood by the nest. They all looked up as I approached.

Without saying a word, I rushed over to the golden nest, reached inside, and carefully wrapped the blanket around the egg. It was my first time touching the egg, and I could feel the strong pulse of life inside. *Please hold on a little longer,* I thought.

Queen Alaina had tears in her eyes when she saw what I had done.

"I made a blanket of sun rays," I said. With Jo's help, I tucked the blanket just right. The egg stopped moving. Maybe it heard my plea.

"You've given us hope," said Queen Alaina. "Now we must send you on your way."

Suddenly the Castle on Stilts began to sway.

"If you are to beat the winds of the storm in order to make it to the other end of the marsh, the time is now!" Queen Alaina said.

"Yes," said Jo. "This blanket is genius, but there's no guarantee how long it will last."

Thunder roared beyond the wall of windows.

Lightning flashed, spidery and menacing across the blackened sky. Then came the wind, a howl as fierce as an ancient battle cry. Jo's bright blue eyes widened. She looked terrified. So did Queen Alaina.

I asked, "What will happen to the other animals and birds of the marsh? Will the shield protect them?"

Queen Alaina exchanged glances with Jo and Hanna. She shook her head. "I fear this storm might mean the end of the marsh."

"Only another force of nature could stand up against the Tangerine Tide," said one of the fairies still working on the shield.

Hanna nodded. "Nature, or those who have the power to manipulate it—that's the only way to redirect this hurricane." She stared intently at me, as though trying to tell me something.

"Whatever happens, we will deal with it," Queen Alaina said, scooping up the egg. "If we don't get you back to the ba-dum boat and on the way now, you won't make it, not before the storm is full upon us."

Everywhere I looked, eyes filled with desperation met mine. Queen Alaina and Jo were desperate to save the crane egg. But Hanna and the Dragonfly Fairies were equally concerned with the marsh.

"What if—" I started.

"NO!" Queen Alaina cut me off. She handed the egg to me. Wrapped peacefully in its blanket of sun rays, the egg felt weightless. Another gust of wind whistled past, pushing at the Castle on Stilts, causing it to groan and shift.

Queen Alaina looked around, her eyes wide with panic. "We've got to move! Let's get Lilu back to the boat. Hanna, Jo, you know what you must do. You know what happens if you fail."

Queen Alaina swooped out the door. She called back to the other Dragonfly Fairies, "Follow me to the ba-dum boat. Bring the shield net. After we see our friends off, we'll need to get it in place."

"Can we at least help you with the net before we leave?" I asked.

"Lilu, there's just no time!" she argued.

"Please, Queen Alaina. You need our help. Let us help with the shield net; then we'll leave. I'll just waste time arguing with you otherwise," I said.

The queen paused, then sighed. "Fine, but let's be quick about it," she said.

I silently celebrated changing her mind, and then glanced guiltily at the egg. This might be a huge mistake, but it felt right to help protect the marsh creatures and fairies. I hoped the baby would understand my decision one day.

I set the egg back in its nest and grabbed an edge of the shield net. Quickly, we dragged it through the castle and out into the wind.

The rain had begun, heavy and fast. Carried by the wind, it tore at our faces, our clothes. It stole our breath.

We spread out across the beach to stretch the net taut. Queen Alaina shouted instructions about how to secure the shield net around the ocean side of the castle.

"We've just about got it!" Queen Alaina yelled. We'd wrapped the net as snuggly as we could. Now we needed volunteer fairies to fly it over the castle to the other side.

I wasn't surprised that Hanna offered to help.

Jo gripped my hand as Hanna took off in the beating rain. We quickly lost sight of her in the darkness.

A horrible ripping sound broke through the crash of thunder. The net had torn! A bright flash of orange showed Hanna caught in the net, being flung around like a rag doll. If we let go of our parts without tying them properly, the net would be lost; but if we didn't help Hanna, we might lose her.

"Save her!" screamed Jo.

Without giving it a second thought, I released my side of the net. So did Queen Alaina.

The net tore in half, and Hanna was flung out onto the beach. She hit the ground heavily.

Jo reached her first. I was close on her heels. Together, we lifted Hanna and carried her back into the castle, where the fairies were regrouping amongst the terrified animals.

"We have nothing to save us now," Queen Alaina said. She turned to Jo and me. "You have to go! If you hurry, you can escape the storm when it slows down at landfall. It is the only way."

But what if she was wrong? What if there was another way? I couldn't give up hope.

With rain pouring down my neck and soaking my bones, I could think of only one thing—saving the marsh.

Queen Alaina and her Dragonfly Fairies had kept the crane egg safe for its parents. Now the fairies needed someone to take care of them.

I had another idea, but it would take weaving something a lot bigger than a blanket, and I didn't know if I could do it. But I knew one thing: I had to try!

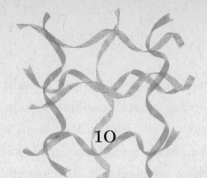

10

Weaving Moonbeams

Hanna groaned. She was coming around after the beating she'd taken out in the elements. I was relieved.

"The early rains have come," Jo said. "Ahead of each storm we get a warning storm. The winds and rain will cease shortly. The dark magic will be next."

"Lilu," Queen Alaina said, "Jo's right. This is the final prelude. To be certain of saving the crane egg, you must leave immediately."

"But what if—"

"You can save the marsh?" Her question came out high-pitched, frantic. "What if you can't?"

Inside the dimly lit Castle on Stilts, the blanket gave off the warm glow of sunset. The egg's shell looked more fragile than ever, but at least for now, the crack had not increased.

How much more time did we have?

Queen Alaina drew a deep breath. "Lilu, the fact that you are here and willing to help is of great comfort, truly. But please understand, we have all sacrificed and taken great pains to protect this egg. We have grown attached to it. Just like in your world, here certain cranes are very rare indeed."

Something inside me, I didn't know what exactly, made me start toward the door. Queen Alaina and the rest of the marsh needed help, and my family had a history with the Moon Goddess. We were known for doing impossible things.

"Hanna, Jo, I need you. Come on!"

Queen Alaina and some of the Dragonfly Fairies yelled for me to come back, but I couldn't stop now. I was out the door and down the steps again. Over my shoulder, I glanced back. Jo was right behind me. Hanna—still recovering—moved a bit more slowly behind her.

"I'm going to talk to the moon," I said. I almost laughed. It was hard to believe that wasn't even the craziest thing I'd said all day. I turned back around before I could see their reaction.

Down on the beach, I planted myself on my knees in the sand. The wind kept roaring. I had to act fast.

I reached into my pocket and grabbed the totem. Hanna and Jo stood aside as I held it up and the lion's mouth began to shine. I'm sure fairy dust fell around me, but in the rain, it was impossible to tell. Out of nowhere, a crazy zigzag of lightning ripped across the sky, but no thunder followed. In fact, the lightning seemed to stop in its tracks. A tall silhouette of a woman wearing a silvery-white crocodile skin appeared before me. She held her face in profile and gave me a sly smile. An ethereal glow surrounded her. The lightning trembled and then melted back into the clouds. For the moment at least, I took this as a sign that the storm wouldn't kill me while I was outside in the elements.

"Why are you calling on the Moon Goddess, daughter of the Songa Lineage?" she asked.

She recognized my family! Her voice was like a bell in a tower tolling the hour. It made me want to move toward her; suddenly I knew how the tide felt. I felt Hanna and Jo walk up beside me, but I didn't turn to acknowledge them. I could only look at the Moon Goddess.

"I would like to use your moonbeams to try to save the marsh from the Tangerine Tide. . . . Please help me, ma'am. Thank you." I bowed my head. She seemed like the type of goddess who deserved every kind of politeness and courtesy.

Her laughter rippled like distant thunder—not scary, but not friendly, either. "What do you know about moonbeams? That's a powerful force."

"Please, ma'am," I urged. "I don't have a lot of time." If she gave me her moonbeams I would make a new shield net, a net big enough to cover the entire marsh.

The Moon Goddess scowled. "When your ancestors needed water, I allowed them to use my moonbeams to pull the tides. The Songa Lineage has always been characterized by strong women capable of extraordinary feats."

She raised her hand and pointed a finger at me. "When I helped your ancestors, I exchanged the moonbeams for their most glorious gift—their baskets. If you want to save the marsh with my moonbeams, you will need to weave them into a stunning basket with a lid to capture the storm's dark magic."

"I—what if I can't—I mean, baskets aren't . . ." I was stammering. "I don't think I have time to make a basket big enough to capture a hurricane." That wasn't the full truth. I just wasn't sure of my skill at basket weaving.

"The basket is your heritage. It's not just made of

reeds, but of the layers of stories and strength and courage of the women who came before you. Besides, if made of moonbeams, a regular-sized basket will expand to hold the dangers of the storm," the Moon Goddess said.

"But I—"

"Enough!" she interrupted. "Be strong and believe in your talents. Do not waste your opportunity. You can never be certain where you'll find opportunity again, especially if you get in the habit of wasting it. Now, you may gather your moonbeams."

She began to glow a cool white light. Just like with the Sun God's rays, I lifted my hand to shield my eyes and broke the light up into beams. Then I pulled on the beams. At first they felt like warm saltwater taffy being pulled, but they turned cold as I gathered them. In the end the moonbeams were cool and coarse, like icy rope. And heavy.

"Hanna! Jo! I need your help!"

We pulled and pulled until the moonbeams formed a big ball on the sand. I was exhausted already. The three of us were panting and out of breath.

The Moon Goddess gave me a brief nod and faded to blackness.

This was it. I had everything I needed now. My

muscles ached. *Why did it have to be a basket?* I could be here on the beach for days and never get it. And I didn't have days. I might not even have hours.

"You can do this, Lilu," said Jo.

"Yeah, we have faith in you," said Hanna.

I noticed a sharp, jagged rock further up the shore. "Help me roll this ball over to that rock," I said.

Together we pushed until the ball was against the rock. Then, using the rock like a pair of scissors, I began to measure and cut the moonbeams until I had several balls all the same size. If I remembered Nan-Nan's directions right, I needed four pieces of reeds going vertical, four pieces going horizontal. Well, in this case, moonbeams.

Unlike the dried grasses Nan-Nan, Mom, and Tan used, the moonbeams were incredibly heavy. I got started weaving, but it wasn't long before I realized how much trouble I was in.

"It keeps coiling up into a knot," I said. "I can't get it to stay straight long enough. This isn't going to work!"

"Come on, Lilu. You've come this far. Are you going to give up?" asked Hanna.

I didn't answer. The winds were rising, and the waves were growing larger and larger. I must have been out of my mind to think I could save the marsh.

Each time my fingers wiggled through the thick

moonbeams, the little bit of progress I'd made would fall apart. Had I come this far just to prove to the entire magical universe that I didn't belong in my own family? Despite the wind and ocean air, my face felt hot. Trying to make this basket was stupid. I couldn't do it. It was just like all the other times, when Tan and I would sit with Mom in our living room or with Nan-Nan on her back porch.

I can't do it!

I flung down the moonbeams against the sand.

"It's not working. If we're going to save the crane egg, we need to get going."

Hanna and Jo rushed after me as I raced toward the rickety Castle on Stilts. "Lilu! Wait! Maybe there's another way!" called Jo.

"You don't even want to try?" said Hanna.

I turned. "All I've done is try. I'm not good at this sort of thing. I never was. Maybe it's the universe's way of telling me I'm in the wrong family."

"Or maybe it's Aventurine's way of telling you to stop whining and fight!" Hanna's words struck me in the chest like a fist.

"I am not whining!" I said. Then I winced, because I could hear the whine in my voice. "Don't you see? If Tandy were here, she'd be able to do this, no problem."

"But Tandy isn't here, and Tandy isn't always going to be 'here,' wherever 'here' is. You don't know what an opportunity you have — the chance to be your own person, your own complete person, to not have to rely on someone else," Jo continued.

I said, "Well, maybe if you didn't hate being a twin so much, you might understand. For Tan and me, being sisters, being twins, means everything. We get to share each other's lives."

"You don't want to share, Lilu. You want to live as one person when you were meant to be two. That is as unnecessary as trying to split yourself apart when you're supposed to be one full person," Hanna said.

They both fell silent. Jo took a step closer. "Do you really want to leave here knowing the marsh could be destroyed? Knowing you might have been able to do more?" she asked.

"But what if I fail?" I whispered.

Hanna moved closer. She said, "But what if you don't?"

I glanced up the stairs. I pictured Queen Alaina pacing back and forth. I saw the expectant faces of all of the fairies and animals waiting to hear news of my success or failure. And I imagined the soft glow of the sun's blanket wrapped snugly around the egg. If I wanted to become a fairy godmother, I had to step into the shoes of my ancestors and never quit.

"Come on," I said. I wouldn't back down, no matter what.

I raced over to the unfinished moonbeams. Whenever I'd tried weaving before, I'd always stopped because I wasn't good at it. At least, that was what I told myself. Now, taking up the crisscrossing moonbeams as I tried to work them into the correct shapes, I realized something important: I didn't get frustrated because I wasn't good at basket weaving. I got frustrated because I thought I wasn't good *enough*! Because I wasn't the best.

Diving had been one of the few things I'd tried that I'd been good at from the start. So I told myself that was what I was meant to do forever. What if there were other things I was good at? Or could be good at with practice?

"I will do this the best way I know how. It might not be pretty, but hopefully, it will get the job done," I said.

Going as fast as I could, yet slower than I felt I should, I constructed the basket's bottom and then its sides. Hanna and Jo tugged and pulled and fed me new strands of moonbeams whenever I needed them.

The basket would start out no bigger than a bucket, but as it filled with dark magic, it would expand. At least, that was the plan.

With each gust of wind or howl from the ocean, my fingers twisted and yanked faster and faster. At last I tied the final knot connecting the locking mechanism to the lid of the basket. I sat back to admire my work.

The basket was a mess. Lumpy and uneven on one side. Not at all elegant and beautiful like the ones lining the shelves at Nan-Nan's. Even so, as I balanced the ugly basket in my hands, rather than feeling ashamed like usual when I messed up, I felt happy.

It was the ugliest basket I'd ever seen. But it was the most beautiful basket I'd ever finished by myself.

"How are we going to keep this thing from flying away?" I asked. The wind was whistling now.

"We need some kind of strong magical grass or string," said Jo. "Something that you can use to tie the basket like a kite to the castle."

"What if we had some of that magical saw grass or whatever? Queen Patchouli seemed to be able to make that stuff do whatever she wanted," I said.

The clouds rolled in overhead. It was as if someone took a showerhead and slanted it right at our faces. The raindrops had teeth—tiny, hungry, angry little teeth that made our cheeks sting.

"That's special grass, and it only grows on that side of the marsh. We don't have it over here," said Jo.

Think, Lilu, think!

My eyes shut tight, I tried to will my mind to come up with a solution. If I had a piece of the magical saw grass that I could expand, we might be able to loop it through the basket's handles and tie the ends around the tall stilt beams holding up the castle. A creaking sound came from above. The Castle on Stilts. Winds pressed the house east and west, north and south. The wooden stilts groaned.

Bits of magic were striking the sand around us, making deep craters in some places and creating sand monsters in others. The sand monsters stood about seven feet tall and looked like the kind of creatures a kindergartner would mold out of clay. They were further down the beach and moved at a snail's pace, but I really, really wanted to get back inside the castle. "I have an idea!" I said.

I snatched my crescent moon shell from my neck. Careful not to lose the shell in the wind, I dropped it into my pocket. Then I used my body to shield the necklace string from the wind. Slowly, carefully, I tugged at the two-foot string. Feeding it with my magic, little by little, it began to grow. And grow. And grow.

"You did it!" cheered Jo.

Working fast, the three of us secured the string through the basket and tied it open, but with a knot that could be pulled loose to bring the lid closed. Next we tugged the string further until we could tie it around the stilt legs holding up the unlikely castle.

Finally, we released the basket. It flew into the air and disappeared in the clouds. I'd done my best. Now we had to wait.

11

The Eye of the Storm

When I was about seven, a hurricane hit South Carolina. It was terrifying and thrilling at the same time. I remember how all the grown-ups were running around, putting pale, blank pieces of plywood over windows until it looked like the whole neighborhood had gone out of business.

When the heavy rains first began, my father called them rain bands. That made Tan and me giggle. We tried to picture fat raindrops playing musical instruments. Dad explained that when he said bands he meant rings—circular, rotating rain clouds. He told us that the hurricane had an eye, or a center. He said wherever the eye of the storm came to shore would get the most damage.

We were right in the flood zone, so we had to evacuate. It was scary, but we stayed with Nan-Nan, who lived further inland. When we came home, some of the houses on our street were in shambles—luckily ours survived. But I knew the power of a hurricane, and this storm had magic in it, too. It was creating monsters out there and tearing up the land. How could a misshapen basket stand up to that?

Inside, the castle was silent. So quiet it was as if the storm were going on in yet another world altogether. When we entered, all the birds, animals, and fairies stood facing the door. Staring.

"We did everything we could," I said.

I went to stand by the golden nest. If one of those sand monsters broke in, I was prepared to fight to protect this little guy. I hoped it would be enough.

Queen Alaina smiled at me. "We're lucky to have such a good friend. Now let's wait and see what happens. The Tangerine Tide might try to get in our way, but with each storm, we grow stronger, too, don't we?"

Everyone broke out in a cheer.

I'd figured we'd all hunker down with our backs to the windows, scared out of our minds. Instead, Queen Alaina and several fairies started passing out little cakes and cups of tea and water.

I thought about the crescent moon shell I'd crammed into my pocket. My supernatural person-to-person calling card straight to my sister. I'd managed to fight my way through one of the strangest, most challenging adventures of my life. And I did it myself. I'd always feared going through something so intense without her would make me feel alone and afraid. But I didn't. I felt . . . *free!*

Realizing that made my face burn. I was ashamed. Why did that always happen? Whenever I started feeling really great, part of me loved the feeling and another part of me started feeling terrible. I moved to face a window. My cheek pressed against the glass, hiding my eyes and my feelings. I touched the darkened window with the palm of my hand. Was it wrong to admit that doing something for myself made me feel free? Free of my twin?

I scanned the darkness, remembering how Tan and I had peeked through the blinds at Nan-Nan's house when we were supposed to be safe in her basement. We were looking for the eye. The eye of the storm. We'd been sure we would look out the window and see some huge unblinking eyeball. We never did. Even so, having her close made me feel safe. I never doubted that we'd make it through that storm because I knew we had each other.

Now I was making my way through another storm. On my own. I opened my palm wider against the window. "I love you, Tan," I whispered onto the glass. The words fogged the window. Maybe Tan and I didn't have to do the exact same thing all the time to be all right. Maybe we could be individuals *and* still be twins.

The fog from my breath faded and then returned. New words appeared through the cloudy glass.

I love you, too. Told you. You're the strong one. Always.

The message was from Tan. Tears pooled in my eyes. Happy tears.

No maybes about it; Tan and I were changing. So was Mom. I wanted to be angry with her. I wanted to make her want to get back together with Dad. Now I could see that would mean moving backward. And if we couldn't move forward, we'd never get anywhere.

"Something's happening," said Queen Alaina. She moved to the doorway. "Lilu, come look!"

I went to her side and stared out the door. My huge basket filled the sky. The moonbeams were straining, and little streaks of lightning were escaping through the places where my weave hadn't been very tight.

But it was holding.

I reached out and quickly pulled the string that released the lid and locked it in place.

A huge cheer rose up behind me. Everyone started dancing around.

"We're not in the clear yet," I said. I turned to Queen Alaina. "How long can we contain it? Doesn't it need to burn out somehow?"

"You're right. The basket won't last forever. But the moonbeams will drain the magic from the Tangerine Tide. It will become a normal storm then. A healthy storm. Soon it will start shrinking." She looked over at the crane egg. "And I think I have a use for the wind."

The queen was right, of course. The basket began to shrink immediately, and the sand monsters awakened by the storm died away. There was a lot of orange goop and damage to the beach, but the castle still stood, and we were safe.

By the time we were all loaded back into the ba-dum boat—me, Hanna, Jo, and the crane egg—the horizon was filled with a beautiful red-streaked sunset. *Red sky at night, sailor's delight,* I thought, feeling that this was a good omen for our trip home.

Queen Alaina saw us off. "Thank you for saving the marsh, Lilu. We will always remember your bravery," she said.

"Thank *you*," I said. "For believing in me."

We hugged good-bye and then took up our now-familiar positions on the boat, with Jo at the chimes and Hanna at the djembe drums. The only difference was the makeshift sail stuck into the middle of the boat—a large piece of sea-hardened driftwood and an old sheet.

My basket had shrunk to the size of a small car. It floated in the air behind us. Queen Alaina's idea. "I think you'll be able to use the storm's wind to propel you back to the Willowood much more quickly than you could with drum power," she'd said.

We waved to the gathering of fairies and animals on the shore, and then Jo pulled on the string to release the basket's lid and the wind curled up inside.

We shot off!

Jo's hand was a blur as she rang the chimes to steer us through the marsh. The wind pushed us faster than I could have imagined. Scenery became a blur.

Downed limbs threatened to steer us off course, but Jo dug in her heels and seemed to will the boat in the right direction.

By the time we reached the dark swamp, the sun was completely gone. The moonbeam basket was now the size of a small table. It glowed with enough light for us to see by, and the sun blanket also shone like a lamp, illuminating a path through the trees.

I had been worried about the marsh frogs here. I didn't think I had it in me to weave more perfumed masks at the moment.

I needn't have worried. Jo was on fire. She didn't lessen the wind as we blew through the trees. Her face showed Zen-like concentration. I could've hugged her! But that would have messed up her flow.

"We're going to make it!" I said through clenched teeth. We rounded a bend and swooshed down to a familiar area of the marsh.

Hanna whooped. My whole body felt antsy. I wanted to get there and get the egg to its parents.

Then the Night Bloomers' Cave appeared around a bend. The shore stretched emerald green and beautiful before us. Several birds dotted the shoreline, dipping their feet and beaks into the water. Breakfast time in the sanctuary for winged creatures. I stole another glance at the egg. We just might make it after all.

Zeus and Zandria were right there at the shore, waiting for us. They were surrounded by dozens of birds of all species and colors.

When we pulled up, I quickly but carefully

hopped out with the egg, not bothering to help tie up the ba-dum boat or mess around with the sail.

"Here's your baby," I said, placing the egg before the two parents.

Zandria pulled back the blanket with her beak and inspected the egg for change. She took in the crack in its shell and then carefully rolled it into a nest of soft grasses and twigs. Their other egg was already there. When I moved closer, I saw that the egg had the exact same crack in the exact same spot as the one we'd rescued. I couldn't help smiling.

Get used to it. Twins share everything. Well, almost everything.

Queen Patchouli appeared beside me, or perhaps she'd been there the whole time. She was smiling at the proud parents. Then she looked at me. "Well done, Lilu," she said.

Then we heard it. *CRACK!* The eggs were hatching. Zeus preened his feathers and hopped anxiously toward the nest. Both eggs were cracking, opening at the same time.

When the baby cranes broke free of their

shells, they staggered and hopped a bit, blinking in the sunlight.

Everyone laughed and celebrated. Zeus whooped with thanks, and Zandria nudged her babies, checking that they were healthy and showing them her love.

I looked around for Hanna and Jo. They were easy to spot, jumping around, hugging and screaming, "Wedidit! Wedidit! Wedidit!"

I laughed. They laughed, too. Laughed and laughed, but they didn't let go of each other. They began to twirl, still holding on, until the strangest thing happened. The more they spun about, the more they disappeared; at least, parts of them did. Until finally, only one sister remained.

But which one?

"Oh no!" I cried.

Queen Patchouli placed her arm around my shoulder. "Do not worry, Lilu. This is how it was supposed to be. Jo and Hanna were two halves of the same whole."

The fairy before me stood, her face familiar yet not quite so. She was neither Hanna nor Jo; yet she was parts of both.

"Hi, Lilu. Please don't freak out. I'm Johanna," she said.

"What?" I said.

"I had such a difficult time, always doubting myself, always second-guessing myself, one time I said I thought it would be easier if I could split myself in two. A creature in the marsh overheard my wish and granted it. The only way I could go back to my old self was to help a fairy-godmother-in-training reunite a set of twins. These two crane eggs."

"What?" I said again.

"Sorry I couldn't just tell you about it, but the magic made it so that I couldn't speak of it until I was whole again."

"Wow," I said, then stuck out my hand. "Nice to meet you, Johanna."

She ignored my hand and pulled me into a big hug. "We did it!" she yelled into my ear.

I laughed and hugged her back.

I was still laughing when I sat up in bed.

"What's so funny?" asked Tandy. Then she chucked her pillow at my head.

"What . . . ? I mean, how . . . ?" I blinked.

Outside the window, a Carolina wren sang its good-morning song.

"I think Mom is up. We need to get downstairs.

The movers will be here soon." Tan rolled out of bed with a loud *WHOOMP.*

She was just about to the door when I spoke up. "Tan, I . . ." I trailed off. How should I begin? It hadn't been a dream. It had been an adventure.

Tandy waved me away. "I know. I was there, too. Sort of, anyway."

I threw aside the covers and sat up straight. Something peeked out from under my pillow. I pulled out the crescent moon shell and held it up to show Tandy. "You *were* really there, right?" I said.

"Of course. Being a fairy-godmother-in-training will be great for you, Lilu. I—I'm really proud," said Tandy.

"Me too!" Mom appeared at the doorway. She had a big smile on her lips. She came over to my bed and sat next to me. Tandy sat next to me as well.

"It was so amazing, you guys. I can't believe I got through it," I said. I handed the shell to Mom.

"Of course you got through it. Why wouldn't you?" said Mom, taking the shell from me carefully.

Tandy rolled her eyes and stood up. "Danger! Danger! Unauthorized bonding!" she said. Her arms stuck out in front of her, robot-style.

Mom laughed. She reached out and grabbed Tandy by the back of her T-shirt and pulled her over to my bed. Then like a soft, warm mama bear, she hugged the both of us until we squealed.

"Mom!" yelled Tandy. "I'm well on my way to becoming a Broadway sensation. What if the paparazzi got ahold of pictures of me hugging you like I was a kid or something?"

Mom rolled her eyes at me. "Heaven forbid the paparazzi take pictures of a loving family. You know, loving family photos are the single biggest cause of young starlets ruining their careers."

We laughed some more. Laughing together like that felt really good. So good that for a second, the old me, the one who always had to come up with a cloud to ruin my silver lining, came back. A shadow of doubt crept across my heart. Not something I was making up, though.

"Mom," I said, sitting back from her for a second. "I'm sorry. I know I haven't been the biggest supporter of you and George. I just wanted us to be a family the way we used to be. With Dad."

"But that can't happen, sweetheart," she said gently.

Tandy was sitting on my bed on her knees.

I said, "I know. We can't go back."

"We have to keep moving forward," Tandy said.

"Living in New York will be a great start to a whole new chapter in our lives, girls. Lilu, I'm just glad you are finally ready to see it that way. I hated the idea of you being unhappy," Mom said.

We all sank back onto the softness of the bed. Tandy talked about the stage roles she was dying to play. I shocked everybody when I announced that instead of looking for a diving team, I might shop around for other activities.

"Maybe gymnastics or dance," I said.

"But you've put so much time into diving," Tandy said.

Mom added with a wink, "And we know how you hate to try something new. Especially when you think it might be too tough for you."

"How will I know what I'm good at if I don't try new things?" I said.

Tan placed her hand on my forehead like she was checking for a fever. "Who are you?" she joked.

I reached out and shook her hand. "My name is Lilu Hart."

Not twin or Tandy's sister, I thought. *Just Lilu. Just plain ol' Lilu.*

And for once, being me was more than enough.

Acknowledgments

Weaving has always been a passion of mine. I learned to spin and dye wool and weave it into fine cloth when I was eighteen in Southern California. I was attracted to the African cultures whose basket weaving connected past and future. It is a woman's work to weave the disparate parts of a life into a beautiful or useful thing. I am weaving now as I thank those who inspired this story. As the mother of identical twin boys, I am honored to have learned about their secret language and witnessed the special bond—unlike any other type of human relationship. Thank you, Evan and Dustin, for being mine and letting me know you deeply. Also, thanks to my dear friend Kat Jones for allowing me to be a part of your adoption of an Ethiopian girl. Love grows out of longing for something deeper in your life, a chance to really know and care for someone else. Also, thanks to Sherri Winston and Chelsea Eberly for making this book possible.

And finally, this story is an ode to my love for birds. It is my challenge to girls to take care of the world's waters, allowing amazing species like the whooping crane to live on.

About the Author

Jan Bozarth was raised in an international family in Texas in the sixties, the daughter of a Cuban mother and a Welsh father. She danced in a ballet company at eleven, started a dream journal at thirteen, joined a surf club at sixteen, studied flower essences at eighteen, and went on to study music, art, and poetry in college. As a girl, she dreamed of a life that would weave these different interests together. Her dream came true when she grew up and had a big family and a music and writing career. Jan is now a grandmother and writes stories and songs for young people. She often works with her own grown-up children, who are musicians and artists in Austin, Texas. (Sometimes Jan is even the fairy godmother who encourages them to believe in their dreams!) Jan credits her own mother, Dora, with handing down her wisdom: Dream big and never give up.

Sumi's Book

Coming soon!

Sumi's a fashionista about to learn that she can change more than just her clothes—
she's a shape-shifter!

(Dear Reader, please note that the following excerpt may change for the actual printing of *Sumi's Book*.)

From *Sumi's Book*

"Queen Patchouli has sent Kano to be your guide," Queen Kumari told me. "He knows the ways of Aventurine. It would be wise to listen to him."

Before I could thank her, the fairy queen faded into the wall. I didn't see a crack or an entrance, but I didn't ponder the mystery. Weird things probably happen all the time in magical lands, and I was more interested in my gifts, especially my guide.

Kano was the most gorgeous boy I had ever seen.

He was dressed in a blue tunic belted over a white shirt and gray leggings. The tops of his boots were turned over like a pirate, but he didn't wear a gold hoop in his ear or a skull-and-crossbones hat on his handsome head. With a mop of curly brown hair, large green eyes, and a slightly lopsided grin, he looked exactly like the boy of my dreams.

"Hello, Sumi," Kano said. His voice sounded like melted caramel, smooth and warm. "Are you ready to begin?"

"Yes," I said without hesitation. Now that I knew Aventurine and my fairy godmother heritage were real, I had to do my best to succeed. I picked up my family's talisman—the empty hand mirror—and tried not to think about Okasan's crescent-shaped scar. "Let's go look for mirror shards."

As I spoke, I remembered that Queen Kumari had faded into the cave wall. I glanced around, assuming that an exit would magically appear. However, the ceiling high above continued to glitter with an unbroken blanket of crystals, and the walls remained solid. The puzzle I had dismissed earlier was suddenly crucial.

"How did you get in here?" I asked.

"Queen Patchouli's magic transported me," Kano explained.

"Is she going to transport us out?" I asked.

"No, we're on our own." Kano grinned with boyish enthusiasm. "It'll be fun. Just follow me, and do what I do."

I didn't understand, but I remembered Queen Kumari's advice. Kano knew what he was doing, and

I had to trust him. I gripped the mirror, braced myself, and then screamed when Kano turned into a snake.

Horrified, I jumped back.

The yellowish-green serpent with a black squiggle on its back raised its broad triangular head. "Ready?" the snake asked in Kano's voice.

I didn't have time to answer. A tingling in my fingers and toes became an intense buzzing that spread through my veins like molten metal. My body felt as though every muscle had fallen asleep, the way my foot does when I sit on it too long. Then my bones cracked, and I screamed again.

"Relaxxxx," Kano said. "Morphing issss painlesssss."

"Sheasy fo' 'ou t'shay!" I couldn't talk. My teeth and tongue were changing shape in my mouth.

"Don't fight it, Ssssumi. Your body will automatically copy whatever form I take."

That did not make me feel better. I was turning into an ugly snake, and there was nothing I could do about it.

Have you read the first
Fairy Godmother Academy book?

Birdie's Book

Will Kerka learn the right Kalis
moves in time to save her sisters?
Find out in

Kerka's Book

Will Zally's ability to talk with animals
be enough to save a fairy queen?
Find out in

Zally's
Book

Can't get enough of the Fairy Godmother Academy?

Check out the website for music, games, and more!
FairyGodmotherAcademy.com

The Fairy Godmother Academy is on Facebook!
Become a fan and get all of the latest news
and updates.